THE BIGGEST
BEAR

Emilia, Anzi, the Bear, and the Dream

Paul J.

Cover design by Alex Peltz, Peltz Creative
peltzcreative.com

Visit the author at
SunLightning.com

ISBN: 978-1-7362902-0-0 (PRINT)
ISBN: 978-1-7362902-1-7 (EBOOK)
ISBN: 978-1-7362902-2-4 (AUDIO)

For You.
Leaping into the canvas,
To become
The art
of You

CONTENTS

THE BIGGEST BEAR 1

CONTENTS 1

Acknowledgements 1

1 – The Garden..1

2– GRRRR! 10

3 – Anzi, The Bear, and The Dream 16

4 – Cold Light..23

5 – Bust Out! 28

6 – Adventure with Anzi 43

7 – Ancestors 59

8 – Long Ago 68

9 – Nothing. Ever. Changes...79

10 – Caláco...97

11 – Preparation 104

12 – Bella Luna 112

13 – The Biggest Bear 125

14 – Ashes to Art..136

Epilogue..146

From the Author 148

ACKNOWLEDGEMENTS

There's a Wave that rolls along the river of Creation.
Catch the Wave, dive for the Gold!

Creative influence is everywhere. The world is filled with material!
Yet some stand out who are revealed, in part, and with gratitude, within these pages.

I would like to thank Mollie Traver, Joanne Breidenstein, Geof Hewitt, Renee Ancel, Larissa Schiller, Kathryn Kirsten, and Stephanie Tourles for their editorial reviews, comments, feedback, and encouragement.

You can't depend on your eyes
when your imagination is out of focus

—MARK TWAIN

1 - THE GARDEN

Emilia wiggled her toes, digging them into the soft, brown earth; hands, knees, and feet caked with soil. She stood to admire her work, wiped her brow with the back of her hand, darkening her forehead too. Next to the new baby lettuce were several rows of young vegetable seedlings. Behind them stood mango, papaya, and orange trees. She looked up and squinted into the low rising sun, drinking it in and letting it warm her face for a moment. In the quiet, she tilted her head toward a distant low hum, and then it was gone. She turned back again to her garden.

"Now grow up strong and think green!" She mothered them softly, squatting close and brushing the baby leaves from underneath.

She loved the garden. Year after year it moved her through the cycles and seasons of nature. Her efforts produced something yummy, useful, and valuable for herself and her family. If there was extra, she would bring it to market and earn a little money. Her mind lingered on the mystery of springtime and how all it took to produce delicious, nourishing, and colorful food was a seed and the combined forces of sunlight, water, soil, and air. In a way, she too was the result of just those four simple elements.

Gathering up her tools, she put them in a bucket, and put the bucket in the tool shed. "*Gaaa!*" she yelled, stepping backwards, knocking over the bucket, which knocked more tools and small parts off their hooks and shelves as a pair of birds flew out of the shed. She ducked, but one of them grazed her hair and shouted back, "*Shiiipt!*"

Recovering her balance, she stood on her tiptoes to see the nest perched on top of the window frame. Inside were three little eggs. "*Oohhh,* hello little ones! Don't worry, your parents will come right back!" She quickly picked up all the tools and parts and went inside.

"Good morning, Mama!" She planted a kiss on Mama's cheek.

"Good morning, mija. You're up early!" Mama brought out three breakfast plates, each full with fresh fruit, eggs, and greens for Emilia, Papa, and herself. Anzi, Emilia's grandfather, always fixed his own breakfast, since it was never spicy enough for him the way Mama made it.

"I really wanted to get the last of my garden planted today. Doesn't it look *sooo* good? Almost like I could eat it now!" She swooned at the window then bounced lightly to the table and took a seat on the bench, still looking out toward the garden. Even now, having just turned fourteen, the garden made her feel like a giddy little kid. She's had a garden ever since she could remember. It was the place where time stood still and everything else in the world disappeared.

"Yes! It's beautiful! Eat up now, you don't want to be late for school." Mama put the plate down in front of her.

Half way through her eggs, Emilia jumped up when Papa came in and tugged at his sleeve, pulling him to the window, "Papa! Look! My garden is all in! Doesn't it look *sooo* delicious!?"

"Yes," he smiled widely at his daughter's enthusiasm, "very nice!" Papa rested his hand on her shoulder and soaked up Emilia's pride in her garden. "Good work! Now let's eat, it's getting late!" For Ernesto, there seemed to be fewer and fewer moments like this to share with his daughter.

Emilia sat down, Papa detoured across the table and pecked Arely on the lips before sitting.

Papa had a mouthful of mango when his phone rang. He looked at the number and sat up straight. "The boss!"

"Maybe about your promotion!" whispered Arely, putting her hand on his.

Papa stood and walked outside to talk.

It didn't take long for Emilia to clean her plate. Mama brushed her daughter's long black hair, pulled it back into a ponytail, and clipped her favorite hair tie to hold it. Emilia made it out of a seashell she picked up off the beach. Mama handed her a bag with lunch and kissed her on the cheek. "Have a good day, Emilia!"

"You too, Mama! Bye!" Emilia walked slowly past her garden, admiring her work again with a smile. "Grow up big and strong!" she said, waving her fingers toward her with palms up as if to encourage immediate growth of all her baby greens. "I'll water you more after school!" Then, not because she was late but because she couldn't help herself, Emilia broke into a jog down the road.

Arely joined Ernesto outside. He was still on the phone. "Today?! Why today? Yes, I understand, but, it's been so many years, we didn't think that would still apply... Yes, I understand it's in the contract, but it's so small, how can it matter?... What? Yes! Of course I want to keep my job! What do you mean by that? You know without our cooperation and our land... yes, yes, your land now... yes, I understand... and there's no other way? Hello?" He folded the silent phone and put it in his pocket.

"What is it?" Arely asked, unnerved by her husband's unsettled look.

"They're coming to take it, the last of it."

"No!" she gasped, and clapped her hands to her cheeks, then to her heart, where they lingered before steeling herself. "When?"

"Today."

"*Today*?! Oh no! No, they can't! After all these years?!" She stomped her feet hard on the ground.

"There's nothing we can do. This has been the agreement since the beginning. I don't know why they chose now, but we should feel lucky to have held on this long."

Arely hugged him, then stepped back and planted her feet firmly. "We will fight this!"

"We have all known that this day was coming. Nobody kept any secrets." Ernesto's defensive tone served well to cover his own concern, and the fact that he was helpless against this fate landing at their feet, here, today.

"Yes, I know, but still..." Arely stared at the ground. "We'll have to break the news to Anzi and Emilia."

Ernesto did not sit down again. He looked out the window at his daughter's pride and joy, quickly gulped down his remaining breakfast, put on his jacket, and picked up his bag. "I must get to work, ahhh, before they take that away too." Once out the door, he wiped his face with his hands and steeled himself for the coming day. For the coming many days and years.

Emilia's daily walk took her from home on the outskirts of the village where her family farmed for generations, to the other side of the town green, where the simple clapboard schoolhouse stood. The town's very existence was made possible by Caláco, the coffee company that almost everyone around worked for in some way. She soon passed the field where she worked, glancing at the plot where she had spent recent weeks planting seeds, and where she would be again later today, after school. Small signs posted throughout the field identified each plant variety, when the seed was sown, and progress notes. A billboard at the main entrance declared, "*A new world of opportunity brought to you by your friends at Caláco.*" This was only one of many coffee fields throughout the area, and Papa was the supervisor of local operations. This field and more, she was told, were once owned by Anzi and his family before him.

Arriving at the edge of the park, she plucked a ripe papaya from one of the many fruit trees scattered throughout the village green. Pulling the small folding knife her mother gave her from a satchel tied at her waist, she sliced it open, scooped out the seeds, and slurped a loud, juicy mouthful of its sweet flesh.

Last year, Caláco donated money to expand the park with tennis courts, game fields, and a pool. They weren't finished yet, but the sign read, "*A new world of recreation brought to you by your friends at Caláco.*"

She took her time walking under the tall, green, shady trees, meandering through the circle of benches around the perimeter. People gathered here on weekends when they weren't working, and sometimes there was music in the evening. She walked toward the white, wooden bandstand in the middle of the grassy green expanse, trying to imagine herself living in the times that her grandfather spoke about. Sometimes she would come here after work and just lie on the grass or sit on the bandstand daydreaming. Papa said her imagination was sometimes too wild, just like some of Anzi's stories.

Lingering for a moment to finish her snack, she wiped papaya juice from her face, jumped off the bandstand and jogged the rest of the way to school with her pack thumping on her back.

It was a small school, the only one in her small village, and she loved learning, especially history. Everyone arrived and left at the same time, every weekday. There was a new addition to the school under construction. The sign in front read, "*A new world of education brought to you by your friends at Caláco.*" She dropped her pack in the hall with the others. There was only one thing she didn't like about school.

"Hey, *Meely*," the familiar sing-song taunt was aimed directly at her, "what's up with that crazy old man's *eyeballs?*" From within the safety of his friend group, Toro crossed his eyes and rolled them around with his tongue sticking out through crooked lips. His friends all mimicked him, laughing.

Emilia rolled her own eyes. *Again?* she thought, trying to ignore them. She scowled quietly, squatting by her pack and pulling a notebook out of it. She loved her grandfather dearly and couldn't stand it when people made fun of him just because there was something wrong with his eyes, especially when there wasn't, not really anyway. Mostly though, she hated how powerless she was to defend him, and she seethed inside until the steam blew the lid off her pot.

"Toro, you... you are *such* a... stupid... *taco!*" She stamped her foot and stormed into the classroom while his friends snickered and laughed.

"Hey, *taco*, I got some *cheese* for you!" one of the boys in the gang said and messed up Toro's hair with his hands, laughing as he did.

"Yeah, and here's the sauce!" said Toro's best friend, Pug, who squirted water from his bottle onto Toro's hair, for which he received a playful push, and all the boys doubled over with laughter.

"Hey, Toro, why make fun of her grandfather?" Miguel challenged the offenders from a distance, surprising even himself. "He's an old man, he can't help it!"

"Who asked you, *nerd*?" The gang pushed Miguel up against the wall, poking and jeering.

"Boys! Enough! *Enough*! Get to your seats!" The teacher scolded, shaking his head with impatience, "Ay yi yi! Every day!" and ushered the boys ahead into the classroom.

Miguel stepped clumsily over the giggling Toro's outstretched foot. Dodging the gauntlet of taunts, he sat in his usual seat, just across from Emilia.

"Thanks, Miguel. They are *such* losers!" said Emilia.

"Sure... I think..." he said, rubbing his arm.

"Sorry!" she grimaced and smiled awkwardly.

They had known each other since they were babies. Their families' friendship went back several generations. Seeing Miguel was one of her favorite things about school. Being with him was comfortable, like being with family, only more, and a little different. Other than her grandfather, he was the only one who seemed to understand her.

A loud kissing sound was directed at them, igniting giggles throughout the room.

The teacher clapped his hands and reprimanded with a pointed finger. "Enough, class, enough. Settle down." He took a deep breath. "Now, good morning, let's get started."

So far, nothing set this day apart from any other.

Emilia stayed after school to ask the teacher for more information about the history lesson.

"Well, you can find books at the library here. You know Caláco has recently donated money to the school so that we have more resources, and that includes some new books. If you don't see what you want, let me know and we'll try to find something for you."

"Oh, that would be awesome! Thank you. It's lucky that we have Caláco here, isn't it?"

The teacher paused in thought. "Yes..., it would seem so." He shifted and added, "You know, Emilia, some of our best historical guides are right here in the village. They might even be living with you." With a wink, the corner of his mouth rose in a smile.

"Well, I think you're right, but it's so hard to get him to talk about things sometimes! Maybe he's forgotten it all."

"I wouldn't be so sure. No grandfather can resist a curious granddaughter!"

"Thanks," she smiled at the acknowledgement of her grandfather. "Well, I have to get to work now, but I'll check the library tomorrow!"

"Excellent," said the teacher. "See you tomorrow."

Opening the door at the end of the hall, Emilia was immediately distracted by the commotion. Miguel was on the ground holding his nose with both hands. Toro and his cronies stood by, mocking him. She ran, but by the time she got to him, the bullies had run off laughing with pride in their successful ambush. Others gathered around Miguel, but Emilia was the one who reached for his arm and helped him sit up.

"Are you okay?"

"I will be," he replied in a muffled, nasal tone, bloody hands still covering his nose.

Emilia took a kerchief out of her backpack and put it in place of where his hands were.

"Thankth," he lisped through the blood-stained kerchief over his swollen nose.

"They're all just *bullies*!" Emilia's hackles were up, ready for a fight.

"We should tell the teacher!" one girl said.

"Yeah, they can't just get away with this!" said another, and more voices joined in agreement.

"That'll juth make it worth," muttered Miguel. "Thankth guyth, I'll be okay." He pulled the kerchief away, saw the blood, and put it back over his nose.

His friends helped him stand up, offering encouraging words.

"Good fight, Miguel!"

"Yeah, way to go!" and with pats on the back they all went their separate directions, secretly happy that they weren't the target, at least for today.

Miguel and Emilia walked together to the park as they often did after school.

"Seriously? He punched you in the nose for sticking up for me this morning? Who does he think he is?" Emilia leaned in with determination.

"He thinkth heeth thtronger than me and heeth right."

Emilia smiled and tried not to laugh at his suddenly funny voice.

"Iths not funny!" he tried to be serious, but his voice put an end to the failed attempt.

Emilia put her hand up to her mouth and lowered her head to cover the grin that was creeping onto her face, and they both laughed.

"Ownch! It hurth when I laugh!"

When they reached the bandstand Emilia said, "Lie," Miguel immediately lay down on the bandstand holding his face with both hands before she could finish, "down."

She took the kerchief off his face, rinsed it in the fountain, and wiped away the blood.

"Not so bad, a little swollen, I'd give it a couple days rest!" Emilia tried to lighten the mood. "And no sneezing!"

"Juth don' tell my dad, okay?"

"Okay, but what will you tell him?"

"I dunno, I'll think of thomething."

"We can't just let them get away with it, Miguel! Toro and his gang need to know they don't make the rules around here!"

"Only they do. But I know you'll think of thomething cleber."

"I have to get my tools from home and get to work. You okay to get there on your own?"

"Thure, fine."

She pulled him up to his feet.

"K. See you later!" Emilia sprinted off in the opposite direction of Miguel's shuffle, looking over her shoulder once to be sure he was still moving. When she did, it made her feel a little bubbly inside. She felt grateful for having such a good friend.

She walked up the path to her house as usual, heading for the tool shed as if on auto-pilot, when she stopped cold. Her heart stopped. Her breath stopped. The whole world stopped.

"My... my..."

Mama ran out of the house to meet her. "Emilia!" she called out.

"My garden – MY GARDEN!!" WHAT HAPPENED??!! *WHAT DID YOU DO??!!*" Tears burst from her eyes at the vision of utter destruction. All the ground around their house and down the hillside, everything had been plowed under. Everything that was green this morning was now brown.

"*Emilia*! Please, we tried to stop them. There was nothing we could do! *Please*, Emilia, you know we tried! But we knew this was going to happen one day."

"You –   didn't – try – HARD – ENOUGH! I HATE YOU! I HATE THIS PLACE!"

There was not enough room in the entire world to contain her fury and not enough distance to be found between where she was now and where she'd rather be. She turned and ran. She couldn't hear the cries or see the tears in her mother's eyes. She ran and ran and ran...

2- GRRRR!

"How could they?!" Emilia pounded up the steep mountain trail taking long strides. Her mind screamed, breath deepened, and pace quickened until she was almost running again. Her eyes were swollen with tears and only anger propelled her forward. Climbing into a light fog through dense green woods, the air grew humid and heavy. Ahead was a steep, rocky ledge. She had never been to the top of this mountain, never past the base of this cliff face. She once saw a couple of older boys scale it to the top, but it took more strength and courage than she had. *"I disagree!"* she said defiantly out loud to her own thought. Gritting her teeth, she confronted the cliff, clawing and scratching in vain, rubble falling at her feet, then slipped back against the stone, resigned to letting it win once again. Turning around, she picked up a rock, threw it down the hillside with all her might, then chased it with a scream. She did it again because it felt so good the first time. Mama was right, she knew for years that this day would eventually come, but denied the expectation of it and never allowed herself to think of it as real. She could not accept the destruction of her prized garden because there was nobody, and everybody, to blame.

Physically and emotionally exhausted, she slid down to the ground, sat quietly with her back against the rock and closed her eyes. She inhaled deeply so her breath could catch her. Moist, earthy air engulfed her by the lungful, like it was breathing her instead of the other way around. Forest sounds pressed into her ears. The green canopy rustled overhead with birds and breeze; an occasional dew-drop of water crashed through the leaves, landing with a soft, mini-explosion of soil. Far away, howler monkeys bickered over something unbearably important, bursting with the rambunctious energy of springtime. But Emilia was still. Only the heavy rising and falling of her chest gave her motion.

She stood again with new energy and determination, confronting the rocky obstacle. She looked up to the top, down at her feet, then straight ahead into the hardness. One hand found a hold. Then the other. One foot pushed, the other kicked itself into a stone crevice. The energetic exertion of muscles transformed anger into resolve through sweat and heavy breath. In and out, one lungful at a time, each brought deeper focus and clarity until it was only her and the rock. Left hand, right foot, right hand, each in turn finding a place of stability. Breath seemed integral to the rhythm of her progress. Inhale: release and grip. Exhale: push and up. She gulped air as if it was pure energetic food. She and the rock were of like mind, each known to the other in strength and intention, neither one would yield. Anger wore itself out against the grit of the stone.

Her upstretched hand landed unexpectedly on soft ground, fingers digging deeply without purchase. She felt her torso slip down. Her legs sprang quickly upward to compensate, allowing the other hand a few precious inches to find and grasp the trunk of a small tree. Heart pounding with fear of falling, feet scratching at nothing, both hands now clenched around the tree, she pulled with all her might. She was finally able to lift one knee high enough for a solid connection to the ground and pushed, pulled, and dragged herself up on her belly, then quickly rolled onto her back, pushing against the tree with her feet to gain some distance from the precipice.

She lay there, looking at the sky, exhausted and breathing hard before realizing what she had just done. Sitting up slowly, clutching the tree, she peered over the thirty-foot-tall rock face and stared straight down at her accomplishment. It wasn't really that far, but she earned herself a whole new perspective with nothing more – or less – than all of her determination.

Emilia stood slowly and looked around to get her bearings in this new place. In the past, she imagined this accomplishment would one day be filled with pride and celebration, but instead she felt only mild satisfaction with a strong dose of indifference. A small sound, faintly familiar, floated on the air. Tilting her head, the distant low hum quickly evaporated, along with the forest's mesmerizing spell, leaving an opening for disappointment to run through her once again like ice. People. *How could they be so mean?* Frozen to the ground with clenched fists, she raised her arms and screamed up at the mountainside for as long and loud as she could, the passionate anger of the loss she felt couldn't hold back its fearsome expression. There was no way she could go back, not after this.

The promises Caláco made got everyone excited about the future. It was hard for her to imagine what people did before all the jobs and projects they brought. They seemed to start something new every few months, but none of their projects were finished yet. She recalled the teacher's puzzling look at school when she brought up the name. There was another sign she'd like to put up: "A new world of better living, HA! Through *destroying my garden!*" The thought of it forced a growl that started from deep in her belly; she yanked a tall fern out of the ground.

After all the long days and years of work she did for them, bent over in the field planting and picking coffee beans. She didn't even like coffee. In fact, hardly anyone ever drank the coffee they worked, yet they spent the best part of every day caring for those plants. She resented every last little bean. They would travel the world while she was stuck here in a life smaller even than a coffee bean. *I have got to get out of here,* she thought. *Maybe go work in the city. Anything. Anywhere but here.*

She stroked the feathery fern in her hand. The base of the cliff she had just climbed was where she taught herself to sing. She was too shy to even speak when she was younger, no encouragement could break her open. Her parents were concerned, but she wasn't; she knew what to say when something was important enough for her attention. It was just that most of the things others cared about seemed insignificant to her. Anzi urged her to go up to the mountains where nobody could hear and sing. '*A song can be sung just for you. Sing long, sing loud, sing until you fall in love with your own voice,* he told her. It felt silly at first, but learning to not be afraid of your own self seemed like the best advice she had ever gotten. As for now, there was no song in her. Her back slid down against the tree that had just saved her. She dangled her feet over the edge, sank her head into her folded arms and sobbed.

She had no idea how much time passed and didn't care. The sun was hidden by increasingly dense mountain fog. She inhaled the rich, heavy scent of young plants and fertile soil being exhaled by the planet, and filled her ears with the sounds of mountain life. Digging her hands softly into the ground on each side, Emilia played with the soil, sifting it between her fingers. She loved everything about the soil, the way its many textures felt in her hands and between her toes, the way it smelled in all different weather and seasons, how it held the roots of living things. Most everyone else thought of soil as just dirt, something to avoid and wash off, but she was captivated by the magic it contained to support life.

Energy began to rise again, compelling her to stand up, shake off the tears and move. A narrow, wooded animal trail revealed itself and she started walking, spinning the fern she still held around in her fingers. She began turning over options in her mind. How long could she survive out here? There was fresh water in the stream, fruit trees, and she knew how to forage for wild edibles. Anzi taught her that. There were jobs in the city, she could work at any market with her experience. But there were no gardens there; none to grow, but none to lose either.

Deep down, Emilia loved her family. Mama seemed to understand her, mostly; at least she had a way of making things right in the end. Until now. But Papa made her crazy! They tried to understand each other, but they did *not* think alike at all. Wherever she went, though, she would miss Anzi the most.

Anzi, more than anyone, was her favorite person. He always made her feel safe and important and she was proud that he was part of her life. He was an old man, a keeper of the old ways, the best storyteller in the village, and the oldest member of the village Council. He was... just... old. Like he was born that way. But she didn't always understand him. There was a mystery about him that Emilia caught glimpses of only occasionally and briefly. He knew all the ancient secrets, the stories, and history of the village and practically everyone who had ever lived there. Like the fern brushing along the plants on the trail as she walked, his stories just barely skimmed the surface of an idea, leaving much to the imagination. He moved quickly, teasing with words that grazed against inspiration but left her hanging without closing the circle of his thought. This frustrated Emilia because she *wanted* to know. She loved hearing the old timers' stories, even though sometimes they didn't make any sense to her. She blamed her own inability to think like them, or maybe she just wasn't smart enough, but often wondered if Anzi and the others intentionally made things difficult to understand.

Kneeling by a small mountain stream, her cupped hands filled with water. She slurped it down, then splashed her face and dunked her wrists to cool off. Reaching into her satchel, she pulled out a small leather pouch and rubbed it between her fingers. The simple, spiral, snake-like design decorating it represented the continuous cycle of growth and change on life's path. At least, that's what Anzi had said when he gave it to her. She opened the pouch to inspect its contents. Inside gleamed a collection of teeth. Twenty of them. Over the years, Anzi had saved all of Emilia's baby teeth as they fell out. On her thirteenth birthday, he gave them all back to her in this pouch he made, saying, "*These teeth are a part of who you once were. They will remind you that with every loss comes something new. They will remind you of the younger you who brought you safely to today; and that today, you are responsible to your older self to deliver your best to her.*" She turned the words over in her mind while turning the teeth over in her fingers. Whenever she felt alone and unimportant, like now, she could hear him say, "*In all the world of being, there never was a never-was.*"

You know how when you overhear half a secret conversation and you have to fill in the blanks, but you *know* that you're making up half the story? That's what talking to Anzi was like sometimes.

If she went to the city, would it be like she was never here? Would it erase her life up until now if she started new somewhere else? She didn't really want to go to the city; she would miss Anzi, and school, and Miguel. She felt the belly bubbles again when she thought of him and took another drink. But how could she stay here and live the sad fate of a bean-working worker-bean for a company that destroyed her most prized possession? She exhaled long and loud, and lay down on her back, dangling her feet in the stream. As much as she hated it right now, it was still her life; and the sights, sounds, and smells that surrounded her were part of who she was, part of the multi-textured fabric of the place she called home. It would be hard to leave.

Her life was not so different from everyone else she knew, with one exception: where she was right now on the side of this mountain was the farthest she had ever been from home, and few had ever ventured even this far. Anzi told her about the spectacular views and panoramic perspective from the top. It was still a long hike from where she was now, but she was determined to make it there one day.

Emilia's world grew much smaller today. There was more to explore, but she was out of ideas for the moment. "*With every loss comes something new.*" He was *totally* wrong about *that!* Nothing good could possibly come from today. Everywhere, bullies seemed to be pushing her around! She tried once more to imagine life somewhere else but could not. The tears were coming again, but she defied them this time, wiping them back before they had a chance to escape. Somehow, she would have to make the best of things, or at least learn to live with them. She sat up, brushed the fern over the water, dropped it gently and watched it float downstream.

It was getting dark, and she was hours away from home. Emilia sat up, carefully put the teeth back in the pouch, tied it tight, and put the pouch into the satchel. She always kept it in the safest of places and often carried it with her. Anzi's love filled the pouch with luck which was hers, it seemed at times, for the asking. But not right now.

3 - ANZI, THE BEAR, AND THE DREAM

A heavy, sullen darkness arrived home with Emilia. Keeping her head down, not looking at anything except the path before her feet, she went straight to her room without dinner and without talking to anyone. Mama and Papa were in the backyard talking. She knew they saw her come in and was relieved they didn't try to engage. She lit a candle and sat down on her bed facing the mirror on the door. The orange flower she had picked on her way home and skewered into her hair above her left ear failed to deliver any hoped-for cheer. The bright orange struck hard against the shiny, anthracite colored hair that rested lightly on her shoulders before being drawn down her back in a loose braid. The soft glow of candlelight reflected in dark, still swollen, almond eyes set in her round, mocha face. A face uncharacteristically blank.

She flopped onto her back exhausted, arms outstretched, and closed her eyes. The night air drew its cool, moist blanket up close, but sleep came hard for Emilia this night. The small victory on the mountain was engulfed by resignation to her utterly powerless life, allowing only brief and fitful periods of semi-consciousness. She tossed at her personal loss and turned with the torment of wondering how her father could possibly believe so strongly in something she could not even fathom to be important. And for *what*? To ruin her life, *that's* what! Finally it came: sweet, deep sleep. And another dream.

She dreamt of the bear Calista so often she had become a nighttime companion. The dreams started several years ago and she had come to take these encounters for granted. At first the bear had chased her. She would either wake up in a panic or run away in fear during the nightmare of it, sure she would be shredded by claws and devoured. But once she stopped being afraid, a relationship developed and grew each night they shared adventures. Calista, though, had a way of moving things just a little ahead of her comfort zone.

She woke up shaky and sweating, unable to relax back into sleep. She slipped from bed and quietly tip-toed outside to the porch. Her eyes met the starry sky at the end of a long exhale. At least the stars were still there, all in the right place. That much she could rely on, but she wasn't so sure about anything else.

"No sleep for you either?" Anzi startled her briefly. He was sitting silent and still on the porch in the dark of night, smiling his twinkling, ageless smile. "I am sorry about your garden."

She slumped heavily down in the chair next to him with a long sigh and closed her eyes. "What do *you* dream about, Anzi?"

"Very often I see your grandmother." He leaned in briefly and looked intently into her eyes. "She comes as a *goddess*! We loved each other very much, and we still do, even across the threshold. But she was no goddess, believe me! Just as I am no saint." He laughed and continued, "Your grandmother was very much human while she lived, as are we all. In our togetherness, we found the perfection of the sand." He looked up at the glimmering white points of light against the darkness.

"What do you mean?" Emilia shifted in her chair and searched for clues in his weathered face.

"One small grain of sand, an oyster, much time and effort, and finally, the pearl."

"Oohhh, I get it. You're the oyster, right?" She was happy with herself to have figured out one of his word puzzles.

"An oyster is *two* halves, hinged together," he smiled and cast a quick wink at her. "Two halves work the grit of the sand to reveal the pearl. We are the oyster, the sand, and the pearl all at once! I miss her dearly. We understood what we held for each other. We shared a very special relationship, and we both knew that. We helped each other in the ways of this world and of another. We helped each other to become *more*; more than we could ever be separately, and to discover that which lay beyond our individuality." His tone lightened. "I feel sometimes that we are still very much in a relationship, though just a little different now." Looking back at the night sky he added, "She knew things, your grandmother. She knew this day would arrive for you, for your generation, and for me."

Emilia looked at Anzi in silence, a bit taken aback by his words. He trusted her with this personal and important secret about his wife, and his dreams. Emilia had only a few vague memories of her grandmother before she passed on. Though the family spoke about her often, she had never heard anything this intimate. His sharing meant everything to her, but made her miss not having known her grandmother even more.

"And you?" Anzi continued, "What has woken you this night? I know it is a trying time for you. I am sorry for that. You know that it was not our ground to grow on, though you had that delicious privilege for a time."

"I know, but it's not that. Well, I mean, it is. I still can't believe it's gone! I can't even *think* about it anymore!" She wiped her hands from the top of her head down to her cheeks. "It's the bear, Anzi, the bear again! She's everywhere inside of me! She won't let me sleep!"

"Do you remember the first time she came to you? You were so frightened that you would be eaten alive!"

"I ran and ran!" she laughed.

"Right into your Mama's arms! And you ran for the next week!" His eyes wrinkled into a squinted smile. "Everywhere you went you looked over your shoulder!" He laughed out loud then stopped and whispered, "We mustn't wake your parents."

"Well, I *was* pretty young, and I still believed the story of the angry bear of the mountains who came after people who didn't do what they were supposed to do. But I'm glad I finally told you."

"Yes, well, sometimes people tell stories so that they don't actually need to confront something they might be uncomfortable with. Especially so with parents and children." Anzi rubbed his chin as he spoke.

"Mama and Papa say that a dream is just a dream and what we do when we're awake is the most important thing."

"That is partly correct, Emilia. But your dreams must also be part of your wakefulness. You cannot ignore either. They inform each other. In a way, though, the dream is bigger than your day."

"What do you mean?"

"It is the difference between being *in* a hurricane, and looking *at* a hurricane from far away. Every day you are in the hurricane that is all the storminess of everyday life, and every night you have a chance to see the storm from outside of itself. From outside of *your* self."

"But what does the bear see from there? I don't understand!" Sometimes Emilia felt like a giant, continuous human question mark.

"Perhaps ask yourself instead what *you* might see from within the bear. Dreams would be much easier to understand if the language was familiar. You will need to learn their language of symbols, imagery, feelings. Our bear friend Calista has revealed herself as your teacher, as a very part of you. She showed you who she is; she told you her name."

"Yes. But tonight she tried to get *inside* of me, to take *over* me!" She bent over, clutching her chest emphatically.

"And you pushed her away?"

"Yes, of *course*! She scared me again! She can't have me! I am *me*," she thumped her chest with her fist, sat up straight and checked her voice, "and she can't take me over!"

"And yet she is part of you. What part of you are you pushing away?"

Emilia opened her mouth to respond before the question caught up with her, and when it did, no words arrived in support.

"In the beginning," Anzi reminded her, "Calista chased you for over a year."

"Yes, you kept telling me to stop running, to face her and ask her what she wanted.

"And you did! That was not easy!"

"You said I should try pretending to ask her in the daytime. I was still afraid, but it also felt good, like I got stronger somehow when I could finally do it. I remember she looked me straight in the eyes and said, *Your breath will not break.* Then she hugged me so tight I squished right into her, like we were both in the same skin."

"And your breath did not break, did it? She teaches you the language she knows. You are already inside of her, and she inside of you, and you are still here, living and breathing."

"But what does she want *now*?"

"The secrets of our lives lie hidden, even from our very selves, locked away in dreams," said Anzi.

Emilia clenched her body and let out a frustrated, "Aahhhh, Anzi, why does it always have to be a riddle?"

"You will need to ask her that yourself. I can only guess. But she had to remind you that she is still inside tonight. I do not believe there is reason for fear." He smiled his most comforting smile.

"Do you know, Anzi? Do you *know*?" She stood up fast and leaned into her own question not because she wanted to but because the energy she suddenly felt was impossible to control. Anzi *always* knew, but he never told exactly, just like in a dream! This revelation both frustrated and astonished her. "I want to be *me*, not *her*! It's like she wants to possess me or something!"

"You will be who you are, Emilia. But Calista seeks you out for reasons only she knows. Let her speak to you however she can. Learn from her perspective. Let your night inform your day, and let your day speak to your night. Make time to imagine during your day today, that she is indeed inside of you. Then ask her what she wants, what she sees, what *she* knows that she wants *you* to know. Use your imagination for just a few minutes when you think of it. Then, if you can, pretend to be her."

"*Be* her?"

"*Be* her. What would you imagine that she might say to you?"

These words put Emilia back in her seat. They rattled around her head for a minute or two but she couldn't absorb them. She trusted Anzi. He just always knew. But 'being her' would have to wait. Too many other things seemed more important right now and she suddenly felt overwhelmed.

"What should I *do* Anzi?" She slumped forward with her cheeks in her hands. "Papa works for them and he couldn't stop them," she slumped even lower. "He *didn't* stop them."

"Come now, Emilia, you know there was nothing he could do. This land we are on has been part of our contractual agreement with Caláco from the beginning, just like all the rest."

"I know, but, *my garden!!*" she whisper-screamed as loud as she could, leaning in and tapping her chest. "It was so small! How could it be worth anything to them when they already have so much?" She sank back into the chair and stared blankly for a moment. "I used to think they were good for us. I mean, without them nobody would have jobs, and they build things everywhere. At least they *say* they're going to with all the signs, but nothing ever gets finished! Why?"

"I agree with you, young wise one, but others do not always see what you see. They are each in their own hurricane. They see the hope of progress as the way forward. Caláco managers have been very convincing in selling us that hope. It is sad that nobody ever felt impoverished until they were told that they are."

"Well, maybe some things are better than they used to be," she conceded, "but it isn't happening very fast!"

Anzi placed his hand in hers and looked at her with a mix of love and sadness. "Our bear friend was once revered as a queen, a protective bear goddess from the ancient days. She is still celebrated now, every year! And that celebration is upon us, as you know. But it did not take very long for the men of Caláco to convince us that she held no power. Their promises were stronger than many of us could resist, which made them," he struggled with the words, "stronger... than her."

"Will you tell me more about her, please?"

"You know that she is our spring Queen who comes out of hibernation to breathe life into our crops." Anzi stood slowly, took a few steps forward out from under the porch, and looked up at the stars. "But there is much more to her story I will be happy to tell you another time when sleep does not call so loudly. Come, look!" he pointed upward. "There she is!"

High overhead, the stars of Ursa Major shimmered brightly in the dark sky of the north, the Big Bear, the first constellation she ever learned.

"She leads all the other constellations through their journey," said Anzi

She looked from the velvety black sky to Anzi, then back to the stars, and for the first time, she recognized the starry sparkle of the night as the same sparkle she sometimes saw in her grandfather's eyes.

Anzi spoke, "Those tiny points of light give us a tiny view into what lies beyond the darkness. Night sky is *always* there, consistent, every night and every day of your life, shining even when it cannot be seen." He turned and smiled at her, "A good quality for a hero."

They stood beside each other for another moment, contentedly staring upward, bathing in starlight. Very quietly he spoke, as though he was thinking aloud, "My spirit is strong; this I trust. But to stand alone in the infinite unknown and not be crushed."

Emilia looked up at him as he stared into infinity, not knowing what to think of those immense words.

Breaking free of the mesmerizing spell of the starry sky, he turned and put his hand on her shoulder. "I have seen tremendous growth in you, Emilia. You make me very proud. And though you may not see it, I know that your parents feel very much the same."

This made Emilia soften and smile. She didn't really know what her parents thought most of the time. '*You're too young to understand,*' they said, words that made her roil inside!

"Today will be a busy day. Sleep is the only thing we need to do right now, and we would do well to find it while some night remains."

They both went quietly back to bed where Emilia slipped quickly into a deep, dreamless, welcome sleep.

4 - COLD LIGHT

Sunlight poked at her bleary eyes through the window. The peace of sleep opened to the blur of morning and quickly gave way to the dread of day. Outside her window was now a bleak expanse of plowed up soil. Soon, small green coffee plants would poke out of the ground. She stared at the plot of land her garden once occupied. It wasn't very big, but it was a place to call her own and nurture whatever she wanted to grow each year. The unwelcome invasion forced her head under the pillow with a groan. No more tears would come, they were pointless anyway.

She loved growing food not just to prepare and eat, but to share and trade. The garden gave so much and asked only for the small and happy exchange of care and attention. It wasn't so long ago when nearly everyone in the village had a big garden or small farms with animals. Each family grew something different and traded or sold the season's bounty among each other and at the market. The community rotated crops and animals each year, adding diversity to the soil, the harvest, and to their personal interactions. Emilia even figured out a system so that the chickens did most of the weeding and kept after the bugs that could quickly destroy the plants. Different crops came in at different times and neighbors helped each other with the harvest and processing. Sometimes a crop failed, but others did well, and with diversity came security. In this way, they grew all of their food and everyone learned to cultivate everything while nurturing both the community and the soil. What Emilia valued most was the feeling of belonging to something bigger, and always having time for fun and adventure. But that was a past that for her existed not so much in memory, but in story.

The village lived in the shadow of Caláco for long enough that it was hard to notice the slow but steady expansion that over time spread itself wide and deep into local livelihoods and village culture. Emilia's family history went back countless generations in this very place, and was a large part of the regional farm network. But that too was in the past. Her garden and the surrounding hillside near their house were the last of the family's land to fall to the hands of the giant coffee conglomerate. With her father's supervisory role in the company, she hoped at least her garden would be spared, but not even he could stop them.

As an accomplished young gardener, Emilia knew that nutrients would quickly be depleted from the soil if a single crop variety were grown in the same place year after year. Unhealthy soil would not be able to support the multitude of living organisms that contribute to healthy soil and plants. To compensate, Caláco would use chemical fertilizers and pesticides to promote maximum yield from their single crop, only to turn the soil into poison for anything else that might try to grow there in the future.

Emilia forced herself to sit up, pulled her work dress down over her head, and shuffled out of the room. She usually enjoyed the morning, but there was nothing to get up for now except the routine and obligation of school and work. Reaching the kitchen where Mama was cooking, she plunked herself down putting her elbows on the table, hands supporting her sulking face. Papa gulped the last of his breakfast.

Mama put a plate of rice, beans, and eggs down in front of her. "Here you are, mija." Emilia was starving but refused to show it.

"You were out late last night Miss mopey. said Papa as if nothing had happened.

Emilia didn't appreciate his attempt at fake cheerfulness. Her entire being cast a sullen frown in his direction as she sat back and folded her arms across her chest.

Papa put down his coffee with a bang. "You can't fight this. These are business matters and that is just the way things are and always will be for us. Time does not go backward, we need to keep up with the world if we're going to compete in it! You might as well get used to it and stop listening to your grandfather's fantasies of the past. Now eat!" He tapped his fork on her plate, emphasizing as he had done so many times that his words were the end of discussion.

"But Papa, it was my *garden!*" cried Emilia, slamming her palms down on the table, rattling everything on it. "How much coffee could grow on such a small piece of ground?!" Her own defiance surprised her more than it did her father; she could read the impatience on his face but held his gaze.

"We need all the cropland we can get if we're to earn any money to live," Papa said sternly. "We've talked about this many times. You knew this was going to happen eventually. Be grateful for what you have!"

"I *hate* money! It's all anyone ever thinks about!" She slumped back in her chair again. "At least when we had the garden we could have fresh fruit in the morning. Now it's just beans and rice. And coffee... from the *worst* of *all* the crops! I hate coffee *too!*" She pushed the plate of rice and beans away as her father took another sip of instant coffee that was produced in a far-away factory and came in a jar.

"It's useless to complain and foolish to not eat," he said, and drank the last of the muddy drink, pushed his chair aside, grabbed his backpack, and called behind him as he left, "I'll see you in the field this afternoon!"

"Emilia." Her mother's comforting voice jarred her from her dour state of mind in a tone she didn't quite believe anymore, but that still offered some small vestige of hope. "I know how you loved your garden. You have to understand that we had no choice in the matter. We can put in another garden one day when we catch up on our bills and pay off our debt so that we can buy some land back. This week, though, I'll need your help to prepare for Saturday."

She had almost forgotten and even forgave her mother for changing the subject. First Saturday, the best day of the year! Emilia always looked forward to this community-wide party when everyone gathered for a feast. For Emilia, the more people who shared a meal, the better it tasted, and this was going to be huge! Things would get started around midday and the talking, laughing, music, and food might last all night. Before supper, the host would introduce issues of importance to the community, and then moderate the village business meeting that followed. After that, the real fun started!

"Good morning, my lovely family!" Anzi was his usual lively, animated self as he entered the kitchen, squeezed Mama's hand, then hovered briefly over the stove inhaling the scent of simmering beans and frying tortillas. Smiling and humming, he reached for some spices on the counter, pinched a little between his fingers, sprinkled and stirred them into the beans, then wafted the aromatic steam with his hand up into his face and leaned closer into the bean pot. "Ahhhh!" he closed his eyes and smiled.

"Good morning, Anzi," said Mama using her forced happiness tone that implied, *I'll try to be patient with you.*

Everyone called him Anzi, everyone except Papa, who just called him "Father" because, well, he was his father.

"Did I hear talk of Bella Luna?" said Anzi.

"What's *that?*" Emilia's head tilted with the question.

"What is the *beautiful moon?* Why, you have been to so many Bella Luna celebrations! I believe this will be your," he counted his fingers and smiled, "fourteenth! Now, tell me you do not know what I am speaking of!" Anzi put his rice and beans on the table, rubbed Emilia's shoulders briefly, and sat down across from her.

"I thought it was called First Saturday," said Emilia.

"It is, Emilia, your grandfather just likes to play with the old language." Mama cast her pursed lips and raised her eyebrows in the direction of Anzi, betraying some mystery that had just been partially revealed.

Mama's reaction did not escape Emilia in the least and she couldn't get the words out fast enough. "What are you *talking* about? What *is* it? Where did it *come* from?"

"Ahh, those were the celebrations to remember! Every month we would gather for the town meeting and full moon celebration. We planned them to be together, and never quite knew what was going to happen or how long things would last." His eyes gleamed until he closed them in memory, a wide smile crept onto his face.

"Really? First Sat... I mean Bella Luna was *every month?*" As usual, Emilia was full of questions.

"Oh, yes!" Anzi quickly came back from his daydream. "But times have changed and now we celebrate only one time each year in the spring, when we also honor the bear reemerging from hibernation as a symbol of the land coming back to life." He winked at her with an extra glimmer in his eye.

"Tell me more!" Emilia finished the last of her breakfast, her own eyes wide with curiosity. She knew there was more to tell about the bear and it seemed he was giving her an opportunity to ask, finally!

Anzi raised up his hand with a pointed finger and opened his mouth to speak.

"Emilia, you must be getting along to school now," Mama interrupted before Anzi could say anything.

She sighed. "Okay, Mama. Anzi, you *will* tell me more, won't you?!" She reached for the lunch bag Mama packed for her and headed for the door without taking her questioning eyes off of Anzi.

"Yes! Of course!" he replied with a smile and another sparkling wink.

Her mood was lifted by the interaction with Anzi, hope reflected in her step out the door. But Emilia kept her head down until she got beyond the ruins of the garden. Worst timing ever for that mess, not that there would ever have been a good time.

This Saturday, Bella Luna would be at their home and Papa would be the host. It would be almost embarrassing to have guests and no garden to show them, just a big, barren patch of ground. Emilia buoyed her spirits with thoughts of stories told by the grandparents who spoke of the old days, family history, flourishing farms and gardens, and the old ways of village life. Hearing about how people once stopped everything to gather at the park *every month* flooded her fertile imagination. She looked forward to the preparations as much as the event itself! But why did Mama interrupt him? And was Calista the bear they honored at Bella Luna the same bear in her dreams? Her mind spun, imagination unraveling thoughts and fantasies like a ball of yarn chased by a kitten.

5 - BUST OUT!

"Hey, *Meely*! Looks like your garden got a *haaaircut*!" Toro and his buddies laughed as she walked into school.

"Yeah, what, you're too *poor* for even a little *gaarden*?" Pug jabbed.

"I am NOT in the mood, *children*!" Emilia looked Toro in the eye while slipping her backpack off one shoulder, not-so-accidentally smacking it into his side as she power-walked past the bullies. This move surprised her as much as them, but her impatience with their immature behavior held her stern attitude together.

"*Ohhh*, a little touchy this morning, aren't we? No kiss from your *booyyy* friend?" The boys all laughed and Toro massaged his side where the pack hit him when nobody was looking.

Emilia kept walking. *Be the bear.* Anzi's words drifted into her head. She was so tired and distracted it left little room to process thoughts or doubt herself. Stopping briefly, mid-stride, she turned to face them and growled with a sneer, cutting through their laughter. It felt good. Their snickering didn't even register with her.

At lunch, she and Miguel sat together outside at the table in the sun.

"It's *gone*?" His mouth dropped open. "*All* of it?" Miguel's nose was still a little swollen but he could speak fine now.

"Yep, just gone. I am *so mad!* I don't even know who exactly to be mad at so I'm just going to be mad at everyone!"

"But..." Miguel looked worried.

"Not *you* of course!" She tilted her head and smiled. "But everyone else could just disappear off the face of the earth for all I care!" Looking down she added quietly, "Especially my father."

"Why do you think they did it?"

"Money! What else? Duh!" she rolled her eyes dramatically.

"Yeah, maybe, but how much money could such a small piece of land puke up in coffee beans?"

Emilia laughed at Miguel's comment and it made her think a little deeper.

"I know, right? The whole thing *does* makes me wanna puke! So how *little* money is it worth to them, or to Papa, to take away the one small thing that was important to *me!?*"

Miguel pointed a knowing finger upward and looked up. "Maybe it's something else."

"*Liiiike??*" She slumped a little over her lunch and held out her hand as if Miguel could simply pour more information into it for her to examine.

"I dunno, but they own everything else around here, so my question is what took them so long to take over your parents' land?"

Emilia was stumped. "Hmm, you might be on to something. Anzi would know, but he is *so* infuriating! Every time I ask him anything he changes the subject or runs out of time or something."

Miguel lowered his voice. "I wonder if he's scared of something. Maybe they threatened your father's job. But I doubt it's about you."

"That's *it*, Miguel! That *has* to be it!" Emilia jumped up, slapped the table, and bounced on her toes.

"What?"

"Power! Money and power. That's all they want! They don't care about *us!*"

"A new world of getting punched in the nose, brought to you by..." Miguel laughed and rubbed his face.

"Exactly! They just punched me and my family right in the nose!" She was half standing, leaning toward Miguel. "They punched the whole town in the nose! And they put up those signs to try and convince us what they *want* us to think. But think about it, Miguel. All the signs and all the projects, and not *one* of them *ever* gets finished!" She slapped her hand on the table again. Miguel leaned back a few inches for safety. "They just dig another hole in the ground and put up another stupid new sign with another *stupid* new lie. Everybody gets excited, but everything gets left in a half-finished heap!" As her words sank in she sat down slowly and started to feel bad for being mad at Papa.

"Woa!" said Miguel. "I think you nailed it! You think we're being duped?"

"*Bullies!* They're *everywhere*! We have to get to the bottom of this, Miguel." Her voice dropped and she slowed her hand before it could slap on the table again. "We *have* to!"

"Emmm?" his voice slow and rising with suspicion, "what are you thinking? I know that look..." He looked down, shaking his head. He knew how impatient she could be sometimes and hoped it wouldn't cause more blood to leak out of his body.

"I don't know, Miguel. I guess I don't really know what to think." She sat back down on the bench. "But who's *really* the boss of everything that goes on around here anyway? Somebody wants control of us, and we don't even know who it is!"

"Village Council? They're the bosses, right?" posed Miguel.

"That's what we've always been taught." Her fervor settled into a tone of scientific inquiry. "That they're looking out for our best interest, but my Anzi is the eldest of all of them; *he's* the boss, and I don't think he would have let them do what they did to my garden."

"Unless," Miguel pondered.

"Unless what?"

"They're trying to hide something?"

"Like *what*? Anzi doesn't always tell me everything, but he wouldn't lie to me." Emilia had always been sure of at least this one thing.

"Let's just ask them this Saturday," said Miguel.

"My father's in charge of this year's meeting. He would kill me if I challenged him like that! So would yours!"

The teacher called outside with the usual signal for afternoon session to begin, "Good afternoon, class!" And everyone shuffled into the building.

30

After school, Emilia found her way grudgingly to the field full of coffee trees. Again. Standing at the edge of the field, hands on hips, she let out an intentionally long sigh with a little grunt at the end. She had about all she could stand of coffee. Once she got started on her work though, the coming weekend took over her thoughts and she didn't notice, much, that she didn't want to be here. The routine settled in all around, the sound of people humming was scattered throughout the field. She hummed along too, then sang quietly, hoping it would help to cheer her. People seemed livelier today. Maybe it was the coming full moon, maybe it was the collective anticipation of Saturday, but she welcomed the happy distraction and the contagion of others' good spirits.

She didn't mind the work so much as the requirement of doing it. After all, it was gardening of sorts, and the soil felt good on her hands and feet. Sometimes she arranged the holes she dug in shapes, and put the beans in to follow the pattern. Singing songs and leaving behind bean art that would never be seen helped to alleviate the drudgery somewhat. But necessity almost always makes things less enjoyable.

Taking a break from bending, kneeling, and crawling on all fours, she stood to stretch her back, leaned on her hoe, and drank in the warm afternoon sun. The big yellow ball melted the huge sky around the village down in the valley, draping it in a shimmering cloak of green and blue.

"Water?" Miguel handed her the jug he was holding.

"Thanks, Miguel. It's so hot out here. Sure is beautiful, though." She wiped sweat from her brow.

Miguel smiled, looking at her while she drank. "It sure is," he said to himself, or at least thought he did. Her eyes moved to his as she lowered the jug, returning his gaze with a half-smile.

"I know you loved your garden," said Miguel, "but me? I couldn't work in the dirt any more than I already do!"

"Soil."

"What?"

"It's soil, not dirt. And it was different. This is *work*, this is *drudgery!* I don't like coffee and I don't know *why* we do it! Except for stupid money." She took another drink and wiped dripping water from her mouth with her arm. "My garden was the *complete* opposite. *My* garden was where I could grow what *I* wanted, what we needed, and we actually ate what I grew!" She reached into her snack bag and pulled out slices of jicama and mango along with a couple of tortillas. Putting one on top of the other, she handed an assembly to Miguel, and popped another in her mouth. "That's all there is. The rest goes into the soup for Saturday."

"Mmm! Thanks, delicious!" Miguel slurped the snack together with his words, "But we just buy what we need at the market." He shrugged and turned back to his work.

Before she could scold him about what he just said, her ear caught the faint low hum again. She shook her head and lightly smacked her ear thinking it was somehow coming from inside of her.

"What's up?" Miguel cocked his head.

"Do you hear that?"

"Hear what?"

"Listen. Listen hard."

"I can barely hear it, like a low rumble?"

"Yes!"

A shot of fear ran through Miguel's face. His voice dropped. "Do you think? Is it? The *bear*?!"

"Seriously Miguel? That's a myth!"

"But..."

"But nothing! *Myth!*"

"What makes you so sure?"

"Anzi." She was steadfast.

Miguel hesitated, "You're old-school, Em!"

"Yes, I guess I *am*!" she turned and jabbed her hoe hard into the ground.

"*No*, I didn't mean it *that* way! I *like* it! You're into all the old ways, like your grandfather, like all our grandparents I guess, and sometimes I know people don't get it but... I..."

Emilia stopped hoeing but didn't look up.

"I think it's cool." Miguel was sincere; she could hear it in his voice.

Still leaning on the hoe, she turned her head slowly. "You do?"

"Yeah. I don't understand it all, but it's cool. Only," he paused in thought and tried to figure out how to say it without it coming out wrong.

"Only what?" she prodded him. Sometimes prodding was the only way to get anything out of him.

"Only... why is he the *only* old-timer who *doesn't* believe that the bear is real?"

"He's not, they *all* know. *Plus*, it's different."

"How do you mean?"

"The bear isn't what we think it is. I don't know how to explain it because they *won't tell us everything!*" Emilia emphasized each syllable with a bang on the ground from the hoe. She simultaneously ran out of words and patience. The noise, the destruction, bullies, work, Papa; all of it suddenly crashed together and punched through her sense of duty.

Looking around while trying not to look like she was looking around, she saw others spread about the vast, sloping field amidst a mix of young plants and taller trees. Some were hunched over their labor putting in new plants, others pruned taller trees. Nobody was looking at her. She turned again to the direction of the noise coming from somewhere over the next mountain and listened hard.

"Emm...? Miguel's voice rose and he tilted his head with concern, "what are you thinking?"

"I'll *prove* it!" She honestly didn't know how she could prove anything, but quiet as the distant sound was, the "bear" inside her called loudly, enticing her imagination. She needed to know, to see it in person. The hoe she was holding beckoned her duty. "*Work,*" she mumbled to herself, now feebly poking the tool at the ground. She couldn't just leave everyone else to do her share of the work; it wouldn't be fair.

"Miguel, is this *all* we are? Is *this* all you want to be?" she said in a loud whisper, waving her arms around the field. "Just another worker-bean making something you don't use, or even like?" The thought went rancid in her mind. "I don't know about you but I, for one," she thumped the hoe on the ground with determination, "want the *truth!*"

"Emilia, what is going *on* with you?" Miguel was starting to get concerned.

"They promise *money*, but we never *see* it! They promise parks and schools and pools, but we never see *anything* ever get finished! They keep all the money they make from what used to be *our* land, and we're supposed to trade *our* sweat, our whole lives, for *their* empty promises?" The world unfolded in her head with the stark realization that up until this moment, she had only a vague understanding of it. Her curiosity suddenly became boundless and uncontrollable. Adventure called her like the sun and rain call the soil to life. She took another long sweeping look around the field.

"They keep saying they're making changes for the better, but nothing ever changes! If anything, it's getting worse!" She scanned the field one more time and crouched low to the ground. "Cover for me!"

"Don't be crazy!" Miguel whispered. "What are you doing?" But she was already moving. "Be careful!" His own words made him feel like a scolding parent and, recognizing this, he sank in his own esteem. He poked at the ground and feigned work while following her quick progress from the corner of his eye, wishing he could go with her from the corner of his mind. She slipped out of sight through the field, rolled under the fence, and disappeared into the trees on the other side. Miguel sent a thought-promise to her that he would be there when she returned, but he knew that this promise was more for himself.

Up the hillside her legs carried her as if they alone were in charge. Ambitious feet cut through the thickening forest toward the steadily growing hum. *Angry bear spirit,* she thought, *What a joke.* It annoyed her that people believed such nonsense and that the grown-ups would keep telling the lie of the story. Her impatience grew with each step. Why didn't everyone know the *real* story of the bear Calista? And especially why didn't *she*? The need to know, to experience the truth of it all, made her ache inside and propelled her ever faster forward. Emilia wanted to know everything about her world, the *whole* world! And she vowed that if she ever had children, she would only tell them the truth!

Sweating as she moved determinedly up the hillside, she grew more frustrated about how Anzi seemed to sidetrack the conversation just when he was getting to the good parts, and how her parents would interrupt them every chance they got. Didn't they trust her with the truth? The taste of desperation landed on her tongue like a single drop of water attempting to quench the enormous thirst of a hot, dry desert.

Lost in wandering thought, one foot knowing only to move ahead of the other, she pushed big leafy branches out of the way, climbed over fallen trees, and jumped streams to blaze a new path. She stopped, closed her eyes, and took a deep breath. She felt a sort of bond between her and the mountain, like she was in the presence of a trusted friend. It felt as if they had been through a lot together, even though this was the first time she had traveled this route.

The air hung suspended, thick with green, and sweet with blossom. The distant roar had disappeared. She only noticed because the silence of her stillness helped to re-focus her attention. She could now hear faint, muffled voices from across the distant valley on the hillside field she left behind. The voices carried on the breeze, sounding out the ancient rhythm of agriculture. She had never heard it quite like this; close enough to recognize the faded melody meandering on a faint breeze, but far enough away that it was indistinguishable. And she—not there singing and working with them. Emilia heard the admonishing voice in her mind as guilt argued with passion. Score one for guilt.

She stood still for a moment. The distant song mingled with nearby sounds of forest life filling the air, swirling around her like leaves in a whirling wind. Perhaps she was hearing things through the filter of fatigue. Note upon note built a new song in her, word upon word amplified and piled up in her mind, slowing to a sonic crawl, they stretched themselves out and danced on the air for her examination. She reached out her arm as if to catch the floating song in her hand, imagining it wrap around and through her fingers. Prying open the space between notes, it felt like peering into a secret dream that could easily envelop her. The song grew and the notes multiplied into a harmony. Each note, each beat, spiraled around and resonated through her, absorbed in turn by the flesh of the trees and the bone of the mountain. In a smooth, crashing wave of recognition, she at once became the music and the trees and the mountain. Like them, she too was also the flesh and bones of the earth.

As if in a trance, time became oddly elastic, eluding any meaning or method of measurement. She didn't know exactly how long she had been gone, and mostly she didn't care. Score one for passion. But thinking caused her bubble to burst with a pang of shame for leaving her co-workers, and so guilt took the lead, but only narrowly. Then she thought of Miguel, maybe waiting for her. Tie score.

The music faded and unraveled from within her daydream, the distant song was silent, and the low droning was gone. She was exhausted and a little annoyed by the fantasy that called her out only to waste her time. With a mix of relief and humility, she turned around and started down the hill to finish the workday. After just a few steps, she stopped dead still in her tracks when ahead came a crash of breaking branches. Her heart skipped a beat and she ducked low, holding her breath. All she could think about was angry bear stories. Another crash, followed by a thud and a curse. She recognized the voice immediately and stood up slowly.

"Miguel?" she called.

"Em? Where are you?"

"Over here!" She stood up and quietly giggled when she saw him sitting on the ground rubbing his leg. "Are you okay?"

"I will be, I think."

"How…" she began, helping him up.

"I dunno, I'm just clumsy."

"No, I mean how did you find me?"

"Well, I left just a minute after you did. You're fast! I got turned around and couldn't figure out which way you went. I just kept going up, looking for the hardest possible way," he paused and grinned, "like what you would do, and then I found this." He reached around his back and pulled up his shirt, "And knew I was on the right track." He held his hand open.

"UUhh!" She grabbed at her waist in disbelief, patting it all around from front to back. "My satchel! It must have come loose along the way! Oh, thank you, Miguel!" She tied it securely around her waist with a double knot. "How did you get away? Did anyone see you?"

"Nah, I go around pretty much unnoticed. I just went under the fence like you did. So, what did you find?"

"Nothing," she sighed. "I guess it was all in my head. All this talk about bears is starting to get to me."

"All *what* talk? I only mentioned it once."

Emilia stumbled for words. She wasn't ready to reveal her dreams or talks with Anzi to Miguel yet. It seemed a little too weird. "Just, well, I guess just that we were talking about it before."

"We still have time to get back before the whistle blows. I bet we can sneak in without being seen," said Miguel as they started down the hill.

"I bet..." she was interrupted by a sudden but distant roar that pierced the veil of the mountain's magical timelessness.

"*What the??!!*" they exclaimed in unison, jumped with adrenaline, then ran in the direction of the noise. It took a few minutes to get to the edge of a steep drop down the mountain that offered a view through the trees and across to a far valley.

"*No. Way!* Miguel! Can you *believe* this?"

"Let's get out of here!"

"NO!" She grabbed his hand and pulled him down to squat and hide behind the brush.

In the distance, the huge monster bellowed smoke. Its single, giant claw scratched hard at the ground, tearing out deep and wide chunks of earth with each scrape. Controlling the big yellow beast was a tiny speck that appeared to be a human sitting in the center of it. There were two other human specks nearby and a small building at the edge of the clearing. Several more machines farther away came alive, humming loudly in the distance, all of them felling trees in a single swipe and churning up billowing clouds of tortured soil. A terrible stench carried uphill on the breeze.

"Who *are* they?" asked Emilia.

"And what are they *doing?*" asked Miguel.

"And *why* are they doing it?" added Emilia.

They looked at each other and simultaneously exclaimed in a loud whisper "*Caláco!*"

This was not some mythical monster. Watching the damage inflicted on the land brought Emilia equal amounts of rage and fear. She turned to Miguel and said, "Why would *anyone* ruin this beautiful place that feeds us?"

"They've gone absolutely insane!" replied Miguel. "Think of all the animals running away from this!"

"And the water! Without the trees the soil will all turn to mud! This is our *home*! How can they *do* this?" Emilia's anguish seethed to the surface. She realized that things were far worse than she could have imagined. If they kept this up, it wouldn't be long before every piece of ground, everything familiar and everything still unknown to her, got turned up and destroyed forever by those growling, smelly, smoking, mechanical abominations. She could not contain all the rage inside of her. She stood up straight and tall and from deep within her belly rose an agonized shout that rang through their ears like a roar.

"*Emilia!*" Miguel grabbed her hand to pull her back down into cover but she turned and ran, frantic feet landing precariously, chased by the ghosts of an unspoken past and the fear of an unknown future. Miguel was right behind her. They didn't stop until they got back to the coffee field.

Ducking low as they emerged from the woods, they wiggled themselves under the fence and slipped quietly, unnoticed, in between separate rows of trees. Emilia wished that she could plant her own self in the ground: a little brown bean left alone to simply grow. Both the sun and the workers' restless actions told her it was almost quitting time. She and Miguel both knew to keep their heads down so as not to call attention to themselves. After only a couple of minutes, Papa blew his supervisor's whistle indicating that it was quitting time. She straggled behind the crowd to avoid talking to anyone, even Miguel, who was a little ahead. Filing past the gate she saw that Papa was busy again, as usual, in the small trailer office, head down and occupied with paperwork. His office trailer was a lot like the one she saw from a distance at the edge of the clearing.

Outside, Emilia soon caught up to Miguel. She tugged on his sleeve, turned abruptly and sped up their pace. Arriving at the edge of the park where they were alone, she stopped and turned, looking at him intensely, and with conviction said, "There is no bear!"

"What? What do you mean?"

"The stories are just stories. We just saw it, the "so-called" bear. It's all been a bunch of lies." Emilia's voice was calm and clear with the truth.

"Right, lies." Miguel tried to follow. "You mean like the stories they told us about the bear were just to keep us from doing bad things when we were kids?"

"And it's worse than I thought! *Why didn't he tell me??!!*"

"What's worse, the bears? Who told you? I mean... didn't tell you? What are you *talking* about?" Miguel took a half step backward with a concerned look.

"Ca-*loco*! They're crazy loco! Their stories are *lies*! The *bear* is named *Calista*, she's a myth from our ancient past, Anzi told me! *She's* the bear and she's *not* a monster! They *stole* her from us! Now they tell us that *she's* the monster! It's *all - lies*! Their *machines* are the monsters! *They're* the monsters and they're cutting down *huge* swaths of forest! *Our* land! We *saw* it, Miguel! They're doing it *right now!* Like they have been for years! I think they plan on taking over *everything!* And all for *money,* for *them!* Nothing for *us!* Not even the trees will be left for us! Or the land or even the water!"

Her agitation animated her so much that Miguel didn't know whether to pay more attention to her words or to her flailing arms; both of which were moving in a dangerous blur. But in the face of her frenzy, Miguel somehow managed to steady his own jittery nerves that took over whenever she was nearby. "Emilia, *slow - down*, just breathe. What does all this mean?" He reached out his hand. Emilia took a deep breath, closed her eyes and squeezed his hand. It came as a surprise to Miguel that he could actually be a calming influence on her because usually *she* was the one calming *him* down.

Her tone became measured and deliberate. "It *means* we're going to be trapped here pushing beans into the ground and pulling them back out for the *rest* of our *lives*. They'll make who we are disappear! Everything that we ever were. There won't be *anything* left of us."

They stared at each other for a moment. Emilia's face was twisted, Miguel was tongue-tied. He hadn't ever really considered his future, taking for granted that it would be spent here in this village that he loved. Everything he heard, thought, and felt right now was completely alien to him. They walked to the bandstand in the empty park and sat on the edge of the stage. He worked to understand Emilia's words. But more importantly, he wanted to understand how he woke up this morning in a world he thought he knew, but now he found himself in a completely foreign land. And he most definitely did not want to let go of her hand.

"This is crazy, Em."

She yanked her hand out of his with a scowl.

"Not *you!* I mean, all of this," he pleaded with his voice and his waving arms. "I just don't understand it all. What did your grandfather tell you? What else do you know about the bear?"

"Don't you see, Miguel? Calista the bear was a big part of our history until she was captured and criticized, made into a scary children's story and left in the dust of so-called *progress*. Ca-*loco* is systematically eliminating our celebrations and traditions, even our *time!* There's so little time for telling stories now that we spend so long working *their* fields that we've forgotten who we are, our history, who *she* is! And nobody seems to notice. Or if they do, nobody wants to do *anything* about it! Everyone wants the shiny new toys of money and progress. Everyone but me, it seems." She slumped backward against a railing post and crossed her arms, near tears.

"And me. I'm *with* you, Em. I've heard some of those old stories at First Saturday."

"Bella Luna," she grunted.

"What?"

"It wasn't always called First Saturday. The feast started as a full moon celebration. It was *every month*, not every *year!*" Her mood brightened a little to tell the story and she sat up straight, happy to share this knowledge with him. "That's how it got its name, but they changed it from what it *really* was!"

"No way! Really?"

"Yep, it was called *Bella Luna*. But they wanted to turn *our* celebrations into *theirs*, so they started calling it First Saturday."

"Woah! This is all starting to make sense now that you put it all together like that. You're lucky to have your grandfather. He has a good memory, but..."

"But what?" She looked sideways at him.

"Wellll...." He was doomed. There was no way out. It was too late.

"I know, you can say it. Go ahead, everyone else does. You think he's crazy too, right? Well, he's *not!*"

"No... I... People totally respect him! You know that! He's like, the chief if we were a tribe, he's everybody's great-grandfather. I guess just nobody *gets* him like you do."

"And *he's* the only one who gets *me*." She slumped back against the post.

"But, Emilia, I *want* to get it. I want to get *you*. I mean, aahh!" He smacked his hand on his forehead and kicked the ground. "That didn't come out right. It's just that I don't understand all of it, not really, but I *want* to. You have to know I'm telling you the truth!"

"I guess I don't understand it all either. I don't know what to think anymore," she sighed in resignation.

"Can you ask Anzi?"

"Miguel?" She stood, facing him, "You're exactly right. If anyone knows anything, it's him. I just need to be a little craftier than he is to get the truth out of him." She picked up both of his hands in hers. "I have to go. I'll see you tomorrow, okay?" Emilia clapped his hands together inside of hers, then turned and ran home, quelling the bubbles in her belly as she went.

The mood at dinner was better than at breakfast, except that she was both absolutely exhausted and bursting with the excitement of questions that she didn't dare ask. Fortunately, Bella Luna planning was a happy distraction for all. Tonight she paid particular attention to Anzi's mannerisms around the fiesta conversation, searching for an angle, something she could use to get him to finally spill everything he knew. She felt like a volcano that was ready, though not allowed, to explode.

After Emilia and Mama had gone to bed, Ernesto approached his father. "She ran off from the field today. I don't know what's gotten into her. I just let her go and blow off some steam."

"The wisest move for a parent is often the most difficult," Anzi offered his support.

"Will you speak with her? She listens to you and doesn't seem to want to hear anything from me lately," Ernesto reluctantly admitted.

"Yes, I will, if you are sure that is what you really want. You and I, our ways can be very different."

"I understand, but I don't know what else to do to reach her and I don't want to lose her. Just talk to her, that's all."

"Very well. She is going through a trying time in many ways, and trust is everything to a young woman."

"Thank you, Father. Yes, I know, and I'm afraid I've betrayed that trust even though there was an understanding with Caláco since long before she was even born."

"It will be difficult to separate your understanding, indeed our understanding, from hers. She has inherited things she is not yet aware of. I will speak with her soon."

"I'm not suggesting that you need to divulge everything. Those details don't matter in our moving ahead. Be discreet with what you share, please, that's all I ask."

"Mmm," grunted Anzi, "There is more to truth than we know how to deal with."

"Thank you, Father. Good night."

"Good night."

6 - ADVENTURE WITH ANZI

In the morning, Emilia stood quietly at his doorway and looked in on her grandfather. Sitting at the edge of his bed, he leaned in close to the small table, flipping through the world on the dial of the old shortwave radio. It was the only technology she had ever seen him use. He said the radio was given to him by a traveler he befriended many years ago. Emilia's friends showed her pictures of the shiny new electronic devices they coveted with touch screens and instant access to everything imaginable. They weren't at all like this big old box with its lights, dials, switches, and hissing static.

The thought of infinite knowledge at her fingertips intrigued her, sometimes insatiably, and it was hard to resist the allure of holding the world of information in the palm of her hand. But something didn't feel right about it; the connection to such an impersonal device seemed weak to her compared to the people and things she could touch, feel, and talk to in her own world.

Anzi fiddled with the dials until the fuzzy squeals became garbled speech, then just barely intelligible. The language was unfamiliar to Emilia, yet Anzi listened intently. With his back to her, Emilia knew he didn't see her, so she started with surprise when he turned and spoke.

"I like to know who we share the world with. Sometimes I can understand what they say, sometimes not. No matter, they are here with us, in different skins with different ideas. I am happy to know of them even if we cannot truly know each other."

"Can you talk to them too?" asked Emilia.

"Oh, yes. My radio friends teach me how other people live and think, how they work and play. Even when I cannot understand the words, language holds the rhythm of their place in the world, and the voices soothe me. Sometimes I try to imagine how their food tastes or what the air might smell like where they live. Listen for a moment to what we share with each other." He leaned back in his chair, pushed his shaggy hair back, closed his wrinkled eyes, and smiled contentedly.

Emilia sat in the chair by the door, quietly trying to hear what Anzi was hearing. A minute passed and the station switched from unintelligible words to music. Anzi stood up, moving toward Emilia doing a little dance shuffle. "Their music is all so very different!" With a spin he mused, "Ahhh! I wish there was more time to learn."

"Anzi, what of *our* music? Will our songs be forgotten?" Emilia was still deeply moved by the scene of destruction she saw yesterday, and she wanted to tell him about it. He offered a hand to Emilia, who took it, and followed his lead.

"As long as you sing and dance, you will carry our music into the future. In fact, I think it will only get louder for you! Beware the voice that does not wish you to sing." He winked, spun her again and they laughed, dancing out of the room into the hall.

The spring in Anzi's step this morning, and his elastic motion belied his age. They landed in the kitchen where her parents were just sitting down to breakfast.

"Emilia and I will be spending the day together," Anzi announced. He moved with conviction; filling his pockets and a bag with food and water as he spun past the table through the house.

Emilia downplayed her surprise and followed his lead, but not quite so enthusiastically for fear of judgement from "the parental eye." She didn't know exactly what to make of his actions, but she knew Anzi's words carried such weight that her parents would not, could not, object.

Papa tried, though, according to his paternal duty. Standing up, he raised his hand and opened his mouth but was instantly and firmly cut off by Anzi before the first syllable could be uttered.

"Too often our potential is lost to requirement! We are off to contrive today's reality!" Anzi was almost giddy as he shuffle-danced to the door, one hand outstretched toward Emilia.

Speechless, Papa waved both his hands above his head in surrender and sat back down with a heavy groan and a slap on the table.

Mama waved them off. "GO! The both of you! So much to be done and you wander off on a lark! Good riddance!" She stood up in frustration and continued muttering under her breath, clearing pots and pans and banging them loudly into the sink. She turned, hands on her hips, staring at Papa with a scowling, furrowed brow. Papa only tapped a fork impatiently on his plate, looking up at the ceiling out of the corner of his eyes. Both of them were resigned to the fact that any effort to change anything Anzi decided to do would be ineffectual.

"*Stubborn old man*" were often the last words of such conversations, and this time was no different, except for the fact that it occurred in complete silence. Emilia kept her head down, not wanting to invite any chance of attention, but managed a meek smile and a shrug in the general direction of her parents on her way out the door.

"That is not how I thought he would handle this," Ernesto muttered to himself after the door closed.

"What do you mean?" His mumblings were often ignored by his wife, but not this time. She knew she was being kept in the dark about something.

The prospect of some unknown adventure ahead with her grandfather lifted Emilia's spirit to rare heights. She hoped it meant that there would be no coffee field to face down today. Together they walked down the road embracing the naïveté of morning, bouncing into the sweet smells and carbonated, green hope of young spring.

After a few minutes Anzi stopped. "Emilia," he looked her square in the eye, "the actions of others will always impact you, as your own actions will impact others. Therefore, it is quite important that you are not *affected* by what others do, and that your conduct is well-considered and true."

She was intent on understanding his unexpected declarations, but this sounded uncomfortably like the beginning of a lecture. The sun sparkled and bounced off Anzi's eyes, making her blink. He turned without another word, and they were off again, making quick time and soon arriving at the park.

"When I was a younger man, we gathered here every afternoon to talk, play soccer, checkers, and music, or just take a nap. The village was smaller then, with fewer people, but most of us came here every day to take a break from our work."

"What kind of work did you do, Anzi?"

"People did lots of different things then, like animal and vegetable farming, sewing and weaving clothes and rugs, building and fixing things, making jewelry, or hammering bowls and utensils out of copper and clay. Everyone pitched in to build and maintain the things and places that belonged to the community: public buildings, this park, our water and energy supply. Always, there was enough to share if somebody was sick or hurt and could not work. Every week we went to the city market to sell or trade our labor and creations. As for me, I did a little of everything and helped however I could. I was very impatient and could never settle on a single expertise. I wanted to learn and try everything!"

"Papa said the jobs that Caláco offers create wealth and an opportunity for everyone to be independent, and that will help grow the village economy and bring progress. But I think I would have liked it more way back then," said Emilia.

"Ohh, yes, I think you would indeed!" Anzi smiled. "Every Saturday night there was music and dancing! This is where I met my Maria! We danced here all the time."

Emilia only had a few fleeting memories of her grandmother. But when Anzi spoke of her, his eyes brightened and glistened, different from the electric blue sparkle they sometimes had.

"Tell me more about those days, and my grandmother!" Emilia was giddy with enthusiasm.

"The old men of the mariachi bands with their big hats, colorful clothes, guitars, and horns played for everyone, but they could spot young lovers easily and play to intoxicate!" The thought made Anzi laugh. "Come now, we have a long way today!"

Anzi was silent and surprisingly fast. Emilia frequently quickened her pace to keep up with him, skip-walking every handful of steps, eventually turning into the woods toward the coast trail.

Anzi stopped abruptly, looked straight ahead, and with a sweeping gesture of his arm said quietly, not to her, but seemingly to the entire forest, "These shadows that grow on the ground, lead us to places unknown and profound." He crossed his arms in an X over his chest, closed his eyes, and bowed his head. Emilia stood close behind him in silence, not completely understanding, but sensing the reverence of his actions.

Lifting his head and stretching out his arms, Anzi scribed an outline in the air with his hands that matched the arched gateway formed by the trees and branches on the trail in front of them. Emilia was surprised to see that the gateway presented a nearly perfect heart shape. She turned to Anzi, eyes wide, mouth open–a speechless, human question mark.

Anzi could only smile. "They are always welcoming, though more so when gratitude is shown for the keepers of places. They have much to teach those who are ready to learn, ready to peel back the next layer of the onion." The cadence of his words gave them the time they required to be heard. "You have many questions, I know. But, Emilia..." he put on his familiar playful grin, "answers are not always easy. Sometimes you will not *know* the right answer, but you will be able to *feel* it. Knowing with feeling," he covered his heart with his right hand and with a big smile, dipped in a half curtsy, "will change your life. And knowing in this way *always* opens to something bigger. I feel that you are ready for that knowing, and for the responsibilities that come with it."

"*Me?!* What responsibility do *I* have? Only to plant those stupid little beans. Look at me; *I* am just a little bean!" She leaned against a tree as she spoke. Her own words and actions made her shrink. She felt like she was going to be asked to do something horribly insurmountable and wished that just once she could keep her mouth shut and stop asking so many questions for which the answers only made things more difficult. Deep down, though, she knew she could never stop asking. Miguel was right, making her life harder seemed to be what she did best. Maybe it would be better to just go back and work in the fields and make everyone else happy.

But she didn't want to disappoint Anzi. The look on her face gave away her trepidation.

"I know you well, Emilia," his comforting tone settled her churning mind. "I will make things right with your parents. Let go of that worry! You are a young woman in a world that you have only a vague knowledge of, but your curiosity is boundless! That is clear to everyone. You will soon own the answers you are looking for. We are much alike in many ways." The comparison gave her a little lift inside and helped her stand a little taller. "You have heard the same calling as I. You can see it in my eyes, and I in yours, we both know it in our dreams. You feel it inside, like a tiny little tickle," he pointed a finger at the center of her chest, "just beneath your doubt," and moved the finger up to the side of her head.

Emilia stood up straight and shook off what seemed now like childish uncertainty, feeling silly for complaining. "I know I want more than to just plant coffee beans, but how do I know what's right for me? It seems like hardly anyone even thinks to ask *what* they want. They just go along with everyone else."

"Think for a moment. You explore our world more than anyone you know. You explore with your questions *and* with your feet. You notice things others do not. *They* wonder why you do, and *you* wonder why they do not. They are reaching *outside* of themselves in search of solutions to what they think of as their own suffering. They have found that money and objects please them and are content to work for those things. So be it. *You* are reaching deeper *inside* for the same solution, a more difficult endeavor with quite different answers. Your eyes and ears are open; they feed your mind with questions. But the mind is a tool for your soul, Emilia. A tool that when strengthened, can help you speak with your heart. No easy trick in a world where most everyone thinks of themselves as their own intellect." He tapped on the side of his head. "The call is faint when you hear your name from a distance. I know too well how easy it is to ignore. Listen hard. You have been called to lead, and leaders must work to gain support."

"A *leader*? *Me!*? HA! You kind of have to be popular to be a leader and I don't even fit in! I don't want what everyone else wants, I don't want progress if it means destroying everything we have! That's not progress, it's death. Death of the village and the memory of everyone who's ever lived here! It's hardly worth all the shiny new plastic junk they want with the money they think they'll earn. I could *never* lead that cause." She began to doubt Anzi's intentions. "I want progress, just not *that* kind of progress." She blushed at the realization of her own hypocrisy. "I mean, I just don't want to be a slave to making money to buy things that don't mean as much as music and dancing with friends in the park. Or my *garden*! It's almost like money buys us *away* from the things that keep us together."

"Yes, a leader in all respects. No more little bean! Ignore the call, and nothing will change; least of all, you. Remember, you are in the eye of your hurricane, but I can see it from the outside. These past days are no accident. If I am correct, you will soon see why. Keep your thoughts and actions true, your spirit strong." He spread both arms wide, spinning around in a slow circle. "And pay attention to *everything*! Embrace that small voice and it will guide you."

"How can you be so *sure* all the time?"

Anzi smiled and mused, "I cannot give away all my secrets! But remember, you are always becoming more than you are. Come, we have lingered enough and it does not take long to grow old, Emilia. When truth is revealed, swift action is essential!" He gestured for Emilia to take the lead down the trail leading deeper into the woods, and they both walked through the green gateway.

Emilia looked back at Anzi briefly every few minutes with a look as if to ask, *Are we there yet? Should we turn here?* But he was deep in thought each time she turned to look. One time she could even see that his eyes were closed while he walked! So she stopped looking back and simply trusted her feet. The woods thickened, making it difficult to see how close the overgrown path was to the cliff above the rocky coast. The rising morning sun filtered sidelong through the mist-engulfed tree canopy.

With the crack of a dead branch underfoot as if to signal his intentions, Anzi took a sharp turn. Emilia spun around to follow and was now behind him. Soon, the ocean filled the horizon far into the distance and about a hundred feet below. Emilia stopped before arriving at the cliff's edge. Anzi did not.

"ANZIII!" she gasped, then let out an involuntary scream as he jumped and disappeared! She sprinted to the cliff's edge where she saw him ducking under the branches of scrubby trees growing out of rock crevices just a few feet below. Her heart was pounding and she shouted again to release the tension, "DON'T *EVER* DO THAT AGAIN!" Unconcerned with her distress, he merely waved and pointed to their destination; the beach far below. She followed him down slowly, carefully.

They made their way through scrubby trees, shimmied down rocks, and hugged the side of the cliff on trails only a little wider than her feet. She moved as fast as she felt safe to move, but Anzi was always just a little ahead of her. *Why doesn't he wait for me?!* She was incredulous at his apparent lack of care for her well-being. And a little amazed at his fearlessness.

"Use the hand-holds on the rocks!" Anzi called out from beyond the other side of a very narrow ledge on the sheer cliff face with a deadly drop just inches away. "They are your best friends right now!"

"*Where are you taking me, old man!!??*" She couldn't believe those words escaped so irreverently loudly from her mouth, but fear and frustration got the better of her good sense as she clung to the cliff, so escape they did. Not quite ready to forgive him, but relieved nonetheless that Anzi stopped to wait for her, she welcomed the reply of his hearty laugh. She made her way slowly across the ledge, trying not to look down and befriending one stone handhold after another. Crouched like a climbing cat against the rocky ledge she glanced over at him, and when she did her foot slipped. "*Anzi!*" she shouted, feeling her body unhinge from its balance point. She clawed frantically at crumbling rocks to regain her grip. Looking down at her doom, she hoped it wouldn't hurt. At once she felt heat and a push at the base of her spine and somehow regained her footing. Steadying herself with a new handhold, she looked at Anzi to see his arm extended toward her, palm open, eyes closed.

"This is not a good time to be a jumping bean!" he sang.

She gripped the rocks more tightly and shuffled more carefully along the cliff edge to the relative safety of slightly more solid ground. She scrambled down the steep trail, hanging on to stunted trees and rocky outcrops, finally landing on the rocky beach where Anzi waited. She looked at him, wide eyed, hands outstretched, mouth open–another human question mark moment–this time in the silent presence of his mischievous grin. He pointed behind her. She was still frazzled by her near fall and so overwhelmed with questions that she had completely forgotten the ocean behind her. The moment she turned to look, a wave crashed over the rocks, soaking them both with spray, reducing her astonishment to humility, and bringing them both to a fit of laughter.

Anzi gestured down the coast. The sun was now high enough to warm and dry them while they walked over rocks and sand. They stopped at a stone formation that stretched from the face of the cliff, across the beach and disappeared into the water. Near the cliff was what looked like a natural doorway shaped into the rock. Again, Anzi drew an air outline of the entrance with his hands before walking through it.

"What *is* this place?! How could I have not known about it? Why don't you *tell* me anything?" she implored, bouncing on tiptoes. They were inside a sculpture carved into the cliff face by eons of being pounded by the ocean. It arched up and over them like a frozen wave flowing out of the rock and moving from land to sea. From the side, it had the distinctive outline of a human ear. They stood on the stone within it that stretched like a bridge allowing water to flow under and around them. On this crystal clear day, the ocean met the sky in a full palette of blues and greens, broken only by the white tops of crashing waves. Emilia looked out to where the water revealed within its depth, many stones, shells, and sea life. She could feel the weight of the water moving, creating a sense of false motion within her.

"Anzi, what...?" She paused. "Why have you taken me here?" She was still awestruck by the dream–like vision of this scene.

"They are not so different, land and sea," he said. "They feed each other, and one to the other is merely transition, a momentary shock, like waking from a dream, or perhaps even like a passing."

"Like... you mean... *death?*" The question mark exposed her insecurity and she turned to face him. "Anzi, you can't... you're not... *you're the only one who understands me!*"

"Ahh, my time here is not yet over," he smiled, looking back out over the ocean. "One day it will be, but not today. Every life is filled with transitions and transformations of one kind or another; best to accept and welcome each as it arrives. Though we may not always appreciate change, we cannot stop it." He bent down and dropped one foot into the water. "Even if the water is cold at first, after a time one becomes acclimated and soon you find it to be exactly what you need."

"Then you don't want to get out!" Emilia enthusiastically finished his thought.

He took her hand and clasped it between both of his, smiling, and nodded, looking into her eyes. "You have my heart, Emilia. I will always be with you, even after I am gone, but my day lies more distant than here. Do not worry. For now, we have work to do."

The sparkle from the sun in his eyes was especially intense here at the seaside. It made her squint and turn her head away. She had never seen it dazzle quite like this, and she knew for sure now that it was more than her imagination or just a trick of the light.

"Anzi, *what* is *up* with your *eyes*?!" Her impulsive words took her by surprise once again, but then so did his. Today has been a very curious day from the start.

He laughed at her expressiveness. "You do have a way with words today. I see it when I look at you as well, and I saw the very same sparkle in the eyes of my own grandmother. It confused me then too, she did not reveal much to me, preferring that I come to discovery on my own terms. But she did take me to see the Bear."

Emilia's eyes could not have opened any wider. She tried to say something, but no words could form on her tied tongue.

"I expect that my parents had the spark too," Anzi continued, stroking his chin with his fingers, "but I cannot be sure. I was an impetuous young man and did not always stop to ask or even to look. But the gift does not always pass to each generation." He paused briefly in thought. "It seems to me that the dignity and grace of our parents, even that of ourselves, are hidden from us under many layers of discovery. Look!" he said abruptly, pointing to the sea.

She didn't hesitate this time, but cast only a distracted glance blindly in the direction of his pointed finger. Dolphins leapt, white ducks dove for food, a wave swelled in the distance. She quickly turned back to face him, aching for more details.

"The Bear? What about the Bear? And the eye thing? What did your grandmother, my great-*great*-grandmother, show you?" She was giddy with questions on the verge of being answered. If she was a balloon, and mysteries were made of air, she would burst if she was filled with just one more.

Anzi continued to stare, apparently mesmerized by the surf, and deep in thought. His eyes reflected the dancing glimmer of sun and sea.

She tore herself away from questions and turned to look. "Let's get out of here!" she cried. A giant wave swelled in the distance, growing and rolling quickly toward them, much bigger than the last. She grabbed his hand and turned to run, but he only tightened his grip and stood firmly, face lit up, looking straight into the coming wave.

"Your breath will not break," he said calmly as the wall of water approached. She squeezed his hand, held her breath, and closed her eyes tight. All she had between life and what looked like certain death was her trust in him.

The wave crested ten feet over their heads and crashed down just in front of them. The water slammed, sprayed, and pounded, forcing itself around and down under their feet within the stone bridge. Its rumbling might tested the foundation of the earth itself. With a ferocious roar, the unstoppable wave was met by the stoic face of the ancient arch in which they stood. The stone absorbed none of its energy, but only redirected the water, pushing it up and around the inside of the stone arch, showering them as it curled back over their heads, wave inside of wave, water inside of rock, and finally sprayed itself back into the ocean. The giant stone ear groaned overhead and underfoot. It seemed to last forever, but it was only seconds before another wave came with equally deafening thunder, and then another. By the time the fourth wave came, Emilia was no longer afraid and both of them were laughing giddily, jumping and stamping their feet uncontrollably, splashing their hands through the water raining over their heads, resonating with the vibrations moving through them. They were thoroughly soaked and in awe of the mighty, deadly, life-affirming power that was being shared with and between them. The stones shook and groaned, ringing low under the stress. Salty rain from each wave skimmed over their heads and it felt now like the water wasn't just splashing *on* her, but moving *through* her like electricity. The tremoring stone reverberated as the last wave receded and the ocean was again calm.

Drenched and laughing all over, Emilia jumped with frantic energy. "How did you *know* about this place!? *Why didn't you show me before!!??* I can't believe we weren't just washed out to sea!"

"I have not *ever* felt that much power here!" said Anzi. "We have had a very special treat! Fast friends, the earth and the sea. They have been doing this dance, feeding each other for many millions of years. Each has given up the fear of being swallowed by the other. When you give up your fear," he looked her in the eyes, "you invite a threat to become an ally. But you must have something to offer in return, or it will never be safe to turn your back on that which feeds you."

They stood in silence for a time, holding on to the experience, incorporating it fully into knowing and remembering, much like trying to hold a dream on waking. She would never forget the feeling.

Emilia broke the silence. "I guess I understand now why you waited so long to show me this. Do you always do that?" She tilted her head inquisitively, "Just wait for the right time?"

"The soup is ready when it is ready. Each ingredient added at just the right time. Choose your moment wisely." He turned around, looking up at the top of the rock arch. "This is the eye and the ear of the world."

"*What?*" Emilia turned to see what he was looking at, glancing back at the ocean as she did.

Standing behind her, Anzi placed a hand on each side of her head, moving it from side to side so she would get the idea, then let go. "Do not look so hard, it makes things more difficult to see!"

She held her breath to steady her gaze, and looked up and through an eye-shaped opening that cut through the top of the stone wave. Moving around, ducking, and squatting, blurring her eyes a bit, she froze and let out a gasp followed by an excited, "OH! No *way!*" At the end of her view, through the portal of the eye, on top of the cliff they had just descended, was a very white statue of a very large bear.

She jumped and laughed in excited disbelief. "Is this for *real?* Anzi, this is blowing my *mind!*" With her hands, she gestured an explosion around her head.

He rolled his eyes, her animation met by his patient and accepting smile. "Yes, for real."

The speechless human question mark didn't know how to respond to this incomprehensible circumstance. "That's the biggest bear ever! Why didn't I see it before?" She stepped out through the stone door, looked up for a better view and rubbed her eyes. "That's weird, I can hardly see it now!" She stepped back in and gazed up through the eye again where the bear was clear and crisp, once she set her focus right.

"What you see and sense here are asleep in the bosom of the earth, awake only to those who have the eye to see." He rested his finger at the corner of his eye, moved it to hers, then pointed up to the stone eye. "When you need to clarify your perspective, come to this place of confluence."

Anzi looked up at the stone eye and moved so that the sun shone through it and landed on his face. Eyes closed, arms crossed again over his chest. Emilia alternately looked out to the sea, then up again in awe-inspired quiet, trying to process all of her sensory input. She felt like a cork bobbing on the ocean surf.

"The bear stands before your ancestors. Come, we will walk."

Anzi's words crashed into Emilia's ears like another wave. The explosion of questions in her mind pulled her away from the ocean back into herself, or at least to some remnant of what she thought was herself. Her head was so flooded she couldn't still her mind long enough to formulate a single question. It felt as though the ocean was trying to give her all of its water at once, but she only had a straw to drink through. All she could do was walk. She held her silence and trusted in the right time. Mysteries were uncovered with each step she made today, and deepened on the next.

Up they climbed, switch-backing to the top of the cliff. For all his years, Anzi continued to move at a pace Emilia struggled to keep up with. When they got to the top, she froze in her steps. Its grandeur overcame her so that a whisper was all she could muster. "Biggest... bear... ever..."

"Perhaps," Anzi replied softly.

She moved slowly, tentatively, toward the magnificent, towering white skeleton of a bear standing watch at the edge of the high cliff. Circling around it, taking it all in, she lifted a hand up to its huge, bony white foot. Her tiny hand covered only part of the paw, and when she touched it she let out a scream, "OUCH!" and jerked her hand back. Her heart was suddenly pounding. "Anzi! I've been bitten by a scorpion!" She turned to run, still looking down at her finger, and froze in her steps mere inches from the edge of the cliff.

"Do not fear where you are not. Be where you are. Here. On top!" Anzi was, as usual, right next to her, smiling. She grabbed his hand with instant and complete relief in its safety. Once she caught her breath, they walked to the other side of the statue where Emilia looked at her stinging hand.

"No bite," said Anzi.

"Then *what*?!" asked the spring-loaded question mark of Emilia.

"You. Calista has reached out to you in your dreams. And now you have met face to face."

"She... she's real!? This is really..." she could hardly say it out loud and whispered in awe, "her? Calista?"

"Do you remember how you felt in your dreams of her? The sting you feel, the buzzing, it is the same, only now it is no dream." He motioned for her to touch the mighty Bear again.

She moved her hand slowly and placed a finger tentatively on the Bear's foot. Again she felt the shock and pulled away. She tried again, this time pushing past the initial jolt, resting her hand more firmly on the bones. The feeling became less shocking and more like holding a swarm of bees, then moved like a warm wave through her body. It reminded her of the dreams where she felt hair – fur – growing quickly out of her body. She held the bony paw tight and closed her eyes, imagining fur growing and feeling the warm energy buzz throughout her body. In her mind's eye she was moving upward, looking down on the figures of herself and Anzi, then out over the cliff to the ocean. It seemed she could see forever and the water was so perfectly clear that everything below the surface readily revealed itself, all the way down to the sandy bottom. The image surprised her so much that she popped open her eyes to find that she was still standing on the ground.

"Anzi! I was so tall! It was like I could see out of her eyes! I could see *everything*!"

He winced and turned his head out of the path of the light that gleamed from her eyes. Anzi put his hand on her shoulder and silently met her eyes with his. She stood strong, tall, tingly, and proud. In his eyes she saw the sparkle, but this time it was different. This time she saw another spark reflected in his eyes, and it was hers. Anzi's deep, resonating laughter came first and soon they both collapsed on the ground, laughing again, uncontrollably.

Sitting up, facing the Bear with the ocean spread wide beyond and below the cliff, Anzi said, "Calista has always been the protector of our village, of us. I have no idea how long she has been standing here. As you now understand, she remains well hidden. But she has given you that sight. *Her* sight. She needs to live and she has chosen to live through you, with you. It won't be easy, we are in a difficult time, a time of transition, of jumping into cold water."

"But why *me*?" It was hard to imagine her question marks getting any bigger, yet they did.

Anzi's tone was determined. "You see. You hear. You understand. Yet you still do not believe. You have made a connection through your intuition, your thoughts, your imagination, your dreams, and most importantly, through your intention, because you *desire* to see and hear and understand. You have, in turn, been seen and heard and understood. Do not ask me how, I do not know. I can only show you what I do know, but it will be up to you to make of it what you will. There is much to learn on your own. You will find yourself here many times I think if your intention remains true."

"But... I'm..." She started to shrink under the weight of it all.

"Do not argue for your imagined limitations!" Anzi interrupted. "The little bean will be yours to keep. Think of it as your seed to nourish and grow in the garden of you. You have been given a great gift! You can see with *her* eyes! But only if you choose to do so. If you say yes to her, there is no turning back. Not that she will trap you, but there will be no other way for you. If you say no, you go back to the beans and live a care-free life of progress."

"I can choose?"

"Of course. This is not a trick or a trap. Nor is it a joke. Anzi stood and reached out his hand to help her up. Both standing now, he faced Calista, arms crossed over his chest again, eyes closed. Emilia did the same.

"What does it mean, the X with your arms?" she asked after he dropped his hands to his side.

"A sign of respectful waiting. Right over left. Intention and willpower over emotion and whimsy." His eye flashed a sparkle at her. "There is more to see. If you choose."

"Are you *kidding?* I'm ready! I am most definitely very ready!" She could hardly believe that there could be more, and could hardly wait to see it.

He nodded and turned in a very decisive walk away from the Bear, back into the woods. It didn't take very long to get there.

7 - ANCESTORS

Anzi stopped abruptly. Emilia waited for him to catch his breath, finally. But he wasn't at all out of breath; he just stood there, looking at her. A smile grew slowly from one side of his face to the other as if revealing the presence of some mystery she wasn't yet aware of. She scanned the surrounding landscape, looking carefully until a gasp leapt out of her. If they hadn't stopped, she might have missed it completely.

A solid green cover of vines and vegetation provided living camouflage that hid the structure in plain sight. Entrancement served to focus her vision. She blinked several times like she was looking at some sort of optical illusion. It was completely overgrown and almost unnoticeable. Its increasing immensity revealed itself at its own pace. Emilia walked slowly from one side to the other trying to take it all in. She rubbed her eyes and shook her head before finally forcing a meek, breathless, "Whaaa... what is this place?"

Anzi was just behind her, standing still, arms crossed again, as if in meditation. Emilia went silent and followed his lead.

"This is the Temple of our Ancestors. It is closely guarded by Calista," replied Anzi.

They moved toward the stairway leading to the entrance. Emilia struggled to master her overwhelmed mind and muscles to walk slowly, gingerly, up the steps. She turned to see Anzi still standing on the ground. "Is this okay?" she asked, hoping she didn't do anything disrespectful. "Are you coming?"

He motioned with his hand for her to continue. "For now, for you."

She turned and continued slowly up the steps, sliding her hand along the mossy rail. Nearing the top, the smell changed from earthy forest floor to something more pungent. Stepping onto the portico she stopped, absent-mindedly scratching at a bump in the green-veiled railing until a hard, brownish material was revealed. She examined it, scratched some more and the brown turned whiter.

"*Bones!*" she exclaimed and turned, wide eyed, to Anzi down below.

"Those who came before us built this temple with the bones of those who went before them. People have lived here since the most ancient of days, and still others before them. No history stands alone. No individual stands alone. What stands here, and what is below, is as old as time itself." Anzi imparted this information carefully and clearly as if he were a school teacher "Older even than I." He motioned for her to continue.

Carefully laid bones made up the walls in a complicated pattern – one on top of the other, some inside of others, some locked together, all the walls were perfectly straight. Wooden beams supported long bones to make the ceiling, flat in some places, arched in others. She walked through the large, open room and then down a dark hallway. Brushing her hand across the walls as she went made her tingle inside. Emilia's imagination raced as she tried to absorb stories from the bones of her ancient ancestors and comprehend the immensity of this unimaginable monument.

On her return to the entrance room, Anzi was there. "Here is where we honor those who unfolded our history, remember those who did not live long enough to know it, and pay respect to those with luck and courage enough to persevere and stay to teach us. Our future is recorded here too; but for now, the past is hard enough to hear."

"It speaks loudly here, Anzi!" her voice reverberated and bounced around the room.

Narrow streaks of light streamed in through small openings in the wall, one ray illuminated an embedded skull. Emilia looked it straight in the eye sockets. Gingerly, she touched it briefly with her fingers in several places, then laid her hands on each of the cheekbones, wondering who it was and what all of their lives were like. She closed her eyes and thought to herself. *Who are you?* Like a movie in her mind, the face filled with flesh and the animation reel ran through an entire day of this past life in only a few seconds. It was something like a visual stream of the stories Anzi told, and not very different from what she imagined her own life would be if not for Caláco's influence. The reality of it went beyond imagination. Startled, her eyes shot open, still staring at the skull as she pulled slowly away from it.

"You see well." Her brief but intense journey did not escape Anzi's sight. Nothing *ever* did. "When you hear that still, small voice, listen carefully. Act accordingly. That is your connection to knowing with feeling."

"It was so real!" Emilia exclaimed.

Anzi nodded. For an instant, his eyes flashed the way and they walked to another stairway leading up to the moss and grass covered roof top. The expansive view spread out beyond the trees to where Calista stood, and on to the ocean. They looked out in silence for a while.

"Emilia, I want all our people to know what our ancestors knew, as do you." Anzi's gaze was intense, directed out to the horizon over the sea, his voice low and humble. "The old ways bore most young people."

"They're not boring to me! But yeah, I guess you're mostly right," said Emilia.

"Well, my generation was no different." Anzi took a deep breath. "This is not easy for me to say, but it is important for you to know. We too wanted to move ahead and grow the community in order to have more opportunities for a better life."

"What do you mean?" Emilia felt on the verge of discovery. She knew that Caláco moved in when he was a young man, but she never heard the whole story.

"We were enamored with the promises and dreams of wealth and progress and so we sold some land to the outsiders when it became valuable. However, we had almost no understanding of the power of money or even how it could be used. This may sound unbelievable to you, but understand that what we needed in those times, we traded amongst ourselves and travelers. Many from my generation were foolish to believe in Caláco's false promises. We did not take the time required to properly understand their contracts. We blindly trusted them to be honest with us and so we signed with our fingerprints, never suspecting they had any reason to fool us. They paid us, but the money was quickly spent and we saw our land, our lifestyle, even our homes plowed away. There is nothing lasting to show for our greed and we are ashamed of the damage caused by our own ignorance. Our children, your parents, saw brief benefits of our dash to advancement because we bought things for them and they became accustomed to those things. Now they remember their childhood with those temporary pleasures, and of course want a good life, a better life, for their children, for you. They do not see that their whole generation has lost connection to the past, to the land, to our stories, and to our great protector, Calista. They know nothing of this place."

Emilia's eyes were transfixed on him. She could hardly believe what she was hearing. The jobs Caláco provided were veiled in vague, ambiguous promises, just like the signs they put up. Anzi sat down on a hard, white bench; long bones of antiquity supporting his flesh. His eyes swelled with trapped tears, and he buried his head in his arms, crushed by the admission of his role in the loss of their community. This sight was as surprising to Emilia as everything else she saw today, but she felt it even more deeply.

They sat beside each other. Her infallible grandfather was, for the first time in her eyes, just a man. And she, just a girl. The prospect of winning back their village and their identity was evaporating like a dream. She understood now why Anzi was so elusive around her questions. The old timers weren't exactly holding back some forbidden knowledge. After what she just heard, it was clear why they wouldn't just come out and admit to selling out their future – her today. Plus, nobody really *wanted* to know! If they did, more people would ask questions instead of just her! If nobody asked, they certainly weren't going to volunteer to reveal their shame. She wanted to be mad at him, at *all* of them. Everyone believed, or wanted to believe, the lies of promised wealth and progress toward a better life. But the past was no better than today. Thousands of years of history, knowledge, and human connection evaporated in just a single generation. It wasn't just Caláco's greed, but their own as well.

Anzi lifted his swollen eyes out of his arm's nest, wiping his face as he did. "Things are just well enough with our lives now so that nobody complains too much. But people do not notice when only one small thing is missing. Soon enough, though, all the tiny pieces add up and everything is lost or forgotten."

Emilia tried to be understanding but her voice shook a little when she spoke. "You did what you thought was best for everyone. It's not your fault they lied and tricked you."

"Perhaps it's not too late!" Anzi perked up. "More than a few of my generation remain, and you have one or two young friends who might want to help," he said with a quick smile. "Perhaps together we can move us all forward."

"What do you mean?"

"My grandmother taught me everything she knew. My mind is strong and memory clear. I know our history, stories, songs, rituals, and all the ancient hidden places, like this! They were part of my life *every day* as a child. But it won't be easy. My generation will need the strength of youth." He looked pointedly at her. "We need to have a *reason* to tell these stories; stories gain strength only when they reach an ear. We need each other to restore truth and breathe life back into who we are."

"Forward into the past!" Emilia exclaimed, punching the sky. "Anzi, will you teach me? Will you teach me what *our* grandparents knew??!" The question mark grew into a mighty, curved tower, stretching up to the clouds and bending over and around to look back at her own self sitting squat just below. The thought of this knowing made her giddy and her heart pounded so fast she had to stand and jump around.

Her enthusiasm made Anzi laugh with delight. "My grandfather, your *great*-grandfather, told me once when I had misbehaved to go outside in the dark and ask the night sky what the moon would say. That is what I asked myself when I realized what we had done, and what it meant for our continued survival. The moon was heavy that day, and she is so still."

He stood up straight and looked out to the horizon, past the distant Bear standing guard by the cliff and recited:

"What would the moon say?
Cresting over poisoned hill,
hanging heavy, still.
She rose up full and round,

and saw without a sound.
Looking down with ancient eye,
she heaved a heavy sigh,
And lost a bit of round."

Reciting those heavy words helped Anzi understand that the only way to remove their weight from his mind was to own his responsibility for them.

"Now with the benefit of time I can say that even if the promised rewards we imagined had materialized, they would not be worth the trade. What promise is worth losing connections among people to the great truths of their roots?" Anzi spread his arms wide and stood, turning around. "We are entwined to each other, bound together by the mysteries shared between ourselves and our great, round world. There is so much yet to learn! It will be difficult to find the time if there is too much busy progress-making."

Emilia had never seen her grandfather as anything but perfect, the one who knew everything, could fix anything, and make her feel special. She understood now that she must bring her own passion and energy into the future she desired to create. As a leader. The thought did not sit easy with her. She liked the idea of a kind of progress that didn't use money to buy independence and isolation, but rather fostered the interdependence of community. Right behind the feeling of satisfaction came a bit of panic as she considered all the pieces that would need to come together amidst the conflict that would surely arise along the way. Papa would *not* be happy! But she knew her only choice was to say yes to this challenge. To *her* challenge. If her grandfather had taught her anything, it was to say 'yes' to life so that opportunity could present itself, and then to accept that opportunity and take action with intention. It was the only path she could see to assemble all the pieces of dreams, bears, and bones. With confidence as immense as the challenge, she knew that whatever it took, it would all be worthwhile if it meant revealing the many things still waiting to be discovered. But all things take time, and it would be important to support those whose lives depended on little beans. She would need to temper her confidence with patience and wisdom to take on this challenge. She needed her grandfather.

"Anzi," she looked at him determinedly. Her new inner confidence took the lead. For the first time she felt like a friend to him, a partner on a journey, not a little nothing bean. "Did you really see the sparkle in my eye?"

"Stronger and brighter than anything! You almost blinded me!" He blinked a sparkle back at her.

Emilia stretched her right hand up high, palm facing him. Anzi returned with a high–five slap and a smile. He took two tortillas out of his pocket and handed one to Emilia, which she was all too happy to take.

"Anzi, will you tell me more about how it came to be? The change I mean, with Caláco." She clasped her hands together in front of her chest. "I really, *really* want to know the whole story."

"That story is still being written, but I will give you my memory of those early days, the first chapter you might call it."

"I want to hear *all* of what you remember! *All of it!*" She was bouncing again, unable to contain herself, the tortilla flopping in her anxious hands. "Don't hold back anything!"

Though he was all too aware of the possibility that she would lose her trust in him, Anzi could no longer deny her enthusiasm or her unfolding potential. The future would be hers, not his. The experiences of today confirmed for him the gifts she possessed. He knew that both of them needed to be fully committed to her receiving those gifts, and that Emilia did not yet fully understand their enormity.

He put both his hands on her shoulders. "Emilia, I will make you this promise. For the remainder of our journey together, I will dive as deep as the need. Now, to your question at hand, even better than telling is showing. That way, you can see and feel and know for yourself. Those days are etched in my memory. Come! I will show you a story."

They walked back through the ossuary and sat on the steps outside. Anzi pulled a handful of fresh, ripe, coffee cherries from his pocket and offered a few to Emilia. "These will help," he said, "I do not really know why, but it does help to settle the stomach."

"UGH! Are you *serious*?!" She scrunched her nose and turned her head. "Get those things away from me!"

Anzi laughed. "Just like your grandmother. These are a little bit different from what you know. My own cultivated hybrids! Try them, they are quite sweet."

Still looking like she had just been sprayed by a skunk, Anzi placed the cherries in her hand, holding back laughter at the sight of her overly dramatic, disdainful grimace. She closed her eyes, trying to pretend they were something more delicious and slowly placed one in her mouth. Then it struck her. Why would he think her stomach needed to be settled? Did he know how she felt about Miguel? Was he going to make *her* talk now? She trusted him, though, and followed his lead.

"I suppose the taste needs to be acquired." Anzi popped a few cherries into his mouth and then took off the leather cord that hung around his neck. Tied to it were four large bear teeth. He wrapped it around his wrist, placing the teeth in his open hand. "Now, hold my hand." Emilia did so without question. Choking down the last bit of coffee bean, she placed her hand on top of his, covering the toothed necklace.

"Are you ready?" Without waiting for an answer Anzi closed his eyes and chanted a short phrase in a language she didn't recognize. It seemed he repeated it three times. He squeezed her hand and she instantly reached out with her free hand to steady herself against swirling stars, wind, and dizziness. Her stomach began to feel a little queasy. Definitely *not* bubbly!

"Do not let go!" Anzi's words came through the whirlwind.

"Not a problem!" she called out.

There was *no way* she was letting go! They were falling down, backward against time, flashes of recent events appeared and faded. Images of mountains, village scenes, rivers, people running about. Many things and people she didn't recognize popped into view and just as quickly disappeared. When the swirling stopped, they landed softly, standing outside in a small, newly planted field. She recognized the little plants as coffee bean seedlings.

"Anzi, *what*...? Where *are* we?" she said, wavering a little, then catching her balance.

"We are in the answers to all your many questions. Because showing is always better than telling. How is your belly?"

"Umm, okay, I guess." She rubbed her stomach.

He handed her a few more cherries, which she chewed not so reluctantly this time. "You will see, in every detail," he smiled, tapping her on the shoulder, "with all the meat on the bones of a story that will satisfy your appetite for knowing. Come and look!" His eyes were sparkling wildly as he spoke, cutting through the misty landscape that veiled them. She followed him across a wooden foot bridge over a river and up to the top of a short hill where they sat on the ground. He pointed, she looked. Two young men were speaking not far away.

"Listen well," he said softly, "and watch closely. It will be as if you are part of the conversation, but they cannot hear or see us."

Emilia gasped. She was already fully engaged and vaguely recognized one of the young men. "Anzi, is that... is that *you*?!"

"Well," he said in a solemn tone, "it is who I used to be."

"*No – way!*" Emilia reeled, looking back and forth at her grandfather, then at the younger Anzi. "How can there be two in the same place?"

"Time is merely a way to separate events so that they don't all happen at once." It seemed so obvious the way he said it. "But I had not yet earned my Anzi back then, you know my parents named me Manuel!"

8 - LONG AGO

The Traveler

"That is really all I can tell you of our history and how it has influenced our lives today. I hope it helps you in your exploration." The young Anzi, Manuel, walked through the small plot of young coffee plants, stopping randomly to examine their growth. The other man followed him closely, scribbled into a notebook, then closed it and slid it into his backpack.

"Yes, Manuel, thank you so much. You and your friends and family have been very helpful and more than generous with your time this past week."

"But I have to tell you, Tomás, there is no future in the way our village operates now," he advised his foreign contemporary in a confident tone.

"What do you mean?" asked Tom.

"Our current organization is based upon simple ways of the past and does not keep with the quickening times of today. Surely you see every day in your country that the world is moving faster by the minute! We must keep up or fall behind!" He stood up straight and smiled. "This!" he said, arms outstretched, turning a full circle, "is our future."

"Of course. The market for coffee is growing exponentially. Do you have a buyer?"

"Oh yes, we have received a very generous offer from a very successful international company. Perhaps you know of them? They have incorporated here under the name of Caláco, the Café Largo Corporation."

"Well, no, I can't say that I've heard of them. A generous offer, you say?"

"Yes, the board of Councilmen have agreed to a very favorable long-term contract. We will sign tomorrow."

"Are you sure you understand the terms?" Tom's tentative tone reflected his concern for the well-being of the people he had come to admire and appreciate for their passionate cultural expressions and the traditions the community held close. The older generation especially embraced their deep history, held a strong connection to the land and nature, and their place in it. There were many things he discovered to be absent in his own life only now, after his visit to this far-away place. His scientific mind struggled with the paradox of missing something he never had.

With a hint of polite defensiveness, Manuel replied, "The managers of Caláco have very carefully explained each point to us. We believe they are acting in good faith and that it will be a mutually beneficial partnership."

"That sounds very good, my friend. I would be happy to review the contract on your behalf and offer another perspective if you wish. You know, some of these companies are just looking for fast money and might take advantage of your situation. I wouldn't want to see that happen to you and your beautiful village."

"I appreciate your kind offer, but that will not be necessary. We have reviewed everything within our Council and have taken the required steps." Manuel's tone was measured to intentionally imply that an outsider's advice would not be needed.

"I apologize. I don't wish to pry into your affairs. But I've seen..."

Manuel put his hand up and took a deep breath, "Your concern is noted and understood, Tomás. We have dealt with dishonest characters in my country as well. Your country is not the only place where one finds unscrupulous business transactions." He softened and put his hand on his new friend's shoulder. "Come, we will share one more meal before you must be on your way."

"I would be honored. Thank you." Tom let the matter drop and they walked together. He was concerned for the village, but more concerned about offending his friend.

"Anzi, who is that? I don't recognize him," asked Emilia.

"You have not met Tomás, but you will understand soon." Anzi pointed as the scene drifted to a small house.

"That's our house!" Emilia called out, "Except without the back part."

"Watch and listen!" Anzi urged.

The Gift

The rich aromas of savory herbs and roasting meat met them along the path home. Manuel led Tom around to the backyard.

"Maria! My love!" He picked up his wife's hand and gave her a dancing spin away from the pot she was stirring over the fire. He elegantly steered her other hand, still holding the spoon, to his mouth and slurped what was left off of it, then landed it back into the simmering stew with a stir, all while still holding her hand. They laughed and embraced, her head against his chest.

Emilia couldn't help the trickle of tears when she saw her grandmother. She was so beautiful. She looked at her grandfather through the mist of time and gripped his hand hard. Anzi smiled and with his other hand, pointed first at Maria, then at Emilia. He whispered in her ear, "You are much alike."

"This is your last evening with us, Tom?" Maria broke the embrace but still held her beloved's hand.

"Yes, sadly. I'll miss your friendship, your beautiful country, and your delicious meals, though I'll be glad to get home to my family and friends."

"Yes, of course you will. You are most welcome anytime you want to visit! And next time bring your lovely wife! I feel I already know her from your stories," replied Maria.

"Yes, indeed, please do!" Manuel grinned mischievously and winked at Maria, who scowled and slapped him on the behind.

Tom laughed, "I'll miss you both. Thank you so much for your hospitality. The bus leaves for the city soon. I'm already packed and set to go."

"I do not care for long goodbyes," groused Manuel. "Hellos and reunions are much more enjoyable."

"Well then, let us enjoy one last meal together, even though it may be a short one," said Maria.

They laughed, ate, drank, and reminisced about the week.

"It's too bad that you can't stay until our celebration next month," Maria offered.

"What celebration is that?" asked Tom.

"Ah, we have discussed this day, the Bella Luna, in our conversations, Tomás," replied Manuel.

"Oh, yes! I will be disappointed to miss that! Next time I'll know to plan my journey with the full moon! It sounds quite special."

"Oh, indeed it is," Maria was animated as she spoke. "Bella Luna is our oldest tradition." She paused and looked at her husband. "As old as the Bear, right Manny?"

"The Bear? I didn't hear about the Bear!" Tom raised his eyebrows in curiosity, spoon hovering in front of his lips.

"Calista is our protectress. She lives deep in the hills." Manuel and Maria shared a deep look of reverence as he spoke of her and she covered his hand with hers.

"Something tells me that's the story I came here for," Tom's voice held hope.

"That tale must await your springtime full moon visit; it is a long story that must be carefully told, and carefully shared." Manuel delivered the blow to Tom who, as an anthropology student, realized his many professional blunders were in part due to poor timing.

"Of course, I understand." Tom hid his cold disappointment behind the cloth he used to wipe the corners of his mouth. He had greatly underestimated the complexity of what he thought would be a simple research project.

Dinner was soon finished, and Tom retrieved his backpack and suitcase from his room. "There's something I'd like to leave for you. Perhaps you'll find it useful, or at least entertaining."

"No, Tomás, please, you do not need to give us anything," Manuel and Maria were almost in unison.

"Well, in fact, you'd be doing me a huge favor; it really is quite heavy and a bit burdensome to carry. I thought I would use it more than I have on my journey." He placed the radio on the table and explained how to operate it.

"Oh, there is no radio here, we cannot use this!" Manuel was reluctant to accept such a valuable gift, yet he was intrigued by what the radio represented in technology, communication, and progress toward a connected world.

"Ah, but one day there will be," Tom persisted, "and this radio is special. It's called *shortwave*, and is able to receive signals from quite far away. You can keep up with news and entertainment from all over the world!" He cranked a handle on the side explaining, "This is how the battery is charged, then just turn on the switch." They all watched closely as the dial lit up. "You'll need to let it warm up for a minute or two."

The radio came to life and sounds emerged through static. Tom tuned the station and adjusted the volume. Count Basie and his Big Band crackled through the speaker. A look of joy lit up Manny's and Maria's faces.

"Wonderful!" exclaimed Manuel with a clap, and the three of them broke into dance and laughter.

"Beautiful!" Maria was ecstatic. "Oh, are you sure?"

"Yes, of course! Ahh, but look at the time," Tom glanced at his watch. "I really must go." He turned down the radio and gave them each a big hug.

"Thank you, thank you very much!" Manuel slapped Tom's back in a warm embrace. "I will most certainly enjoy your gift of the entire world in one small box!" His eyes glittered with a mist of gratitude and Maria watched his reaction intently, a bit nervously, wondering if he might accidentally give away his secret. He quickly wiped his eyes with the cloth in his pocket, but not before Tom cocked his head and gave Manuel a curious, slightly astonished look.

"And I have something for you!" Maria quickly interjected and held out a sealed gourd filled with soup. "You can fit this in place of where your radio was. It's a good meal or two for your long journey home."

Tom graciously accepted the gourd with another hug, for which he received a peck on the cheek from Maria. Manuel put his hand on Tom's shoulder, walked him through the door and outside to the narrow dirt track leading to town.

"Good bye, Tom, and best of luck to you!" called Maria from the doorway.

"Thank you for everything!" Tom called back to Maria and Manuel. With that, he turned and was off to the bus stop, fingers crossed that there would, in fact, be a bus to get on in this tiny town.

"So that's where you got your radio," said Emilia. "I never really thought about it; you've just always had it."

"Yes, and as I recall, that was quite a good year for soup!" Anzi waved his hand from left to right and the story changed again. "I think you might enjoy this. Your grandmother had very good instincts."

The Plan

Manuel rose early, excited for the new day. He went outside to greet the young sun by gazing into its light with eyes closed, face and palms absorbing the rising fire. After a few minutes in this warm and nourishing silence, he picked fruit from a tree, plucked a few warm eggs from under the hens, and started a pot of coffee. He only recently learned to brew coffee from the Caláco managers, who were understandably eager to have the village adopt and enjoy this new beverage.

Soon the coffee, fruit, and eggs were ready. He put them on a tray and brought them to the bedroom where Maria was just waking up. Placing the tray carefully in the middle of the bed, he climbed back into it, kissed Maria, and put a slice of papaya to her lips. She slurped it out of his fingers with a gush. "Ohh, how I *love* papaya!" she exclaimed.

He handed her a cup of coffee. "Ohh, how I *despise* that drink!" she spat, pushing it away. "How can such a sour drink pass over such sweet lips as yours?"

"This drink is our future!" he cried out in exaggerated delight, raising the cup as if in a toast. "A future that begins today! And these sweet lips are your future as well, my lucky love!" He smiled, pausing briefly to enjoy her papaya flavored lips again. "Today we sign our contract and the future grows ever brighter for us." He looked down at her belly, quietly growing under the night dress, rubbed it gently with his hand, then put his head down to listen. "And for our children, too!"

"What should we name our little bambino?" Maria whispered.

"If a boy, I have always liked Ernesto."

"Papa? That's papa in there?!" Emilia was beside herself and started to laugh.

Anzi smiled, nodded, and put a finger to his lips.

"Oh, yes, perfect for you because you are so in earnest yourself!" She tousled his hair and laughed, followed quickly by a sigh, "I'll miss cooking for a guest. There's still so much food, and it's always better shared! I'd like to cook for Gabriela and Philipé tonight!" Maria exclaimed.

"Fine, I do enjoy their company," Manuel said cheerfully.

"You know Gabriela is with child as well, and they've chosen 'Alonso' for a boy. Tonight, we can discuss the names we like for girls!"

"Of course! I look forward to this evening with our dinner guests then!"

"Manny," she started, reaching for his hand, "do you really think this is the right thing to do? Coffee, I mean? And so much of our future committed to it!"

"Maria! I cannot keep up with you! We have been through this before! I thought we were in agreement?"

"I know, my love, but I've been thinking, and I now wonder whether turning over the rights to develop our land is the best thing to do?"

"Everything will come back to us, just as it is spelled out in the contract!" Manuel held his confident, yet patient tone.

"It could take a *very* long time."

"We are doing this to bring a better life to our village! To our children and *their* children! We will not lose anything of who we are or what we have, and things will improve rapidly as we become part of the greater world of international commerce! This is a collaboration that will ease our hardship. Surely you appreciate this, Maria."

"I know, and I understand all of that. But I've developed a funny feeling about it."

"I think it may be the little one inside that is giving you the funny feelings!" He smiled and tickled her belly, which made her smile.

"Promise me this, my Manuel."

"Anything, my love."

She pierced him with an uncompromising and unyielding eye. "You and the other Council members make sure that the contract allows us to keep our traditions and our land so that we will not lose anything."

"All the Council members are in agreement, and share your concerns, as do I." Manny stood and looked out the window at the countryside. "We must move forward, Maria. Things will most certainly change, but *only* for the better." He looked at her with sincerity, "I promise!"

"Come to me," she said, arms open. He did so, and they affirmed their vow to one another.

Anzi quickly swished his arm from side to side while flicking his fingers and the scene dissolved. Emilia giggled. He pointed to a new image and said, "This is where our trouble began. There was more than enough wit, arrogance, greed, and ego for all to feast on. The combined sleight of hand tricked us that day."

The Agreement

The clock on the wall struck 10 AM. The Council members received the Caláco managers in the village office. After the formality of greetings and handshakes, a round of strong drink was poured according to the time-honored tradition when making important agreements. The oldest man on the Caláco team, G. Bigly, Sr., sat next to the youngest member, G. Bigly, Jr. When they sat, Bigly, Sr. opened his folder and was the first to speak.

"Gentlemen, thank you once again for sharing your wonderful village with us. I speak for the team when I say that we all look forward to building a long and prosperous relationship with you!" Glasses were raised and joined with a clatter in tribute to their partnership, "Cheers, Gentlemen!"

"Hear! Hear!" came the reply to the sound of clinking glass and smiles all around the table, followed quickly by another pour.

"Gentlemen of the Council," continued Bigly, "the board of Caláco looks forward to a long and profitable partnership with you. As you know, it will take some years before the full plan comes to fruition and we all realize the maximum benefit of the agreement we are making today. Of course, like all of you, we do this for our families, for future generations." He looked over and smiled at his son, slapped his shoulder, tapped his cigar into the ashtray, and nodded in a way that elicited agreement from his team.

"Yes, of course!" the Caláco men all chimed in.

"Agreed. To our families!" replied the men of the Council.

They all lifted their glasses again and drank to their families and to prosperity.

"However, it has come to our attorney's attention that there is just one small detail we neglected, a mere formality required by our company to comply with international laws for doing business with foreign nations. Not that we consider you to be foreigners, we are like family!" He poured more liquor all around and raised his glass, as did all the others. "To our *new* family!"

"New family!" they cheered again as they drank.

"Of course, I personally apologize for the oversight, but rest assured, gentlemen, these are minor formalities. It's just business. You know how lawyers can be. Surely you understand," he laughed along with his team.

"Does this change the nature of our agreement?" asked the head Councilman.

"This does not change things in the slightest. It merely clarifies language that allows us to move forward, unencumbered, with our plans at a time that is most economically favorable to us, er, rather, to our partnership."

"Please show us the language."

"Of course!" Bigly turned the contract toward the inquiring lead Councilman, flipping pages and pointing out the additions. The team of men leaned over the contract as if to scrutinize the nuance, but the foreign legal language was a jumble of words to them.

"Now," continued Bigly, "we understand that you may need to take your time and look things over, but time is of the essence, gentlemen, and we have been approached by some of your neighboring villages. Though, of course, we would much prefer to do business with you, our new family. Isn't that right, men?"

The Caláco team nodded back and forth, mumbling affirmations at each other. Bigly, Sr. exclaimed, "To our team!" And they all raised their glasses again, tipping the drink back into their mouths.

"And as a gesture of good faith," Bigly continued, pulling the contract abruptly back to his side of the table, "we are prepared to offer an advance bonus payment to your community! You can do as you wish with the money for your town, for your families. We do not need to record this transaction as part of our contractual agreement." He slid a fat envelope across the table.

The head Councilman examined it, nodded his approval to Bigly and then to his board. He tapped his empty glass on the table. "We are in agreement. We thank you for your kind gesture and for your interest in doing business with our community." He refilled all the glasses which were quickly raised, tipped, and slammed down empty on the table almost in unison.

Bigly flipped through more of the contract, and then turned the papers back toward the Council. "We just need a signature there on the bottom."

The head Councilman looked at the members of his team, each of whom nodded in agreement, then across the table at the Caláco team and said firmly, "We all sign, as our ancestors did."

"Whatever you want!" Bigly smiled and handed him a pen.

The head Councilman pulled a feathered eagle talon from his vest pocket, poked his finger with it, and made his mark on the paper. He passed the talon and the contract to the next man, and in turn they each made their mark on the contract in their own blood.

"Mmm, yes, indeed, quite dramatic, Councilmen!" Bigly solicited his board for approval, which they quickly provided in the form of enthusiastic applause and admiration for the Council.

The deal was sealed with one final pour, and the jug was empty.

Back to Now

"And that is how yesterday brought trouble to today. Please accept my apologies; they can never be sufficient to repair what has been damaged. I did not know we were being tricked. I was blinded by my own ambition." He handed Emilia a few more coffee cherries. "For your belly. It is time to return."

Emilia was silent. She didn't know what she could possibly say. She took the cherries and chewed them without any objection.

They joined hands again over the bear tooth necklace, and fell forward again through time with the same spinning, dizzying, windy roar. They landed softly back on the temple steps. Dizzy and a bit queasy, they both slid on their backsides to the bottom step and lay down on the grass, staring up at the sky until their stomachs settled.

"Anzi?" Emilia sat up straight. She felt all the piercing determination she had seen in her grandmother inside of her, and the power of being a partner with Anzi. There was no more little bean.

He turned to her. This time he was the question mark.

"I choose *yes*!"

He picked up her hand and smiled his wide smile. She stood first, helped him up, and they began the journey home in the evening sunset. A giant, quivering, nearly full moon was just now peeking up over the horizon. It would be quite late by the time they got home.

9 - NOTHING. EVER. CHANGES.

Breakfast the next morning was surprisingly quiet. As far as Emilia knew, her parents didn't have a clue about the details of the day with Anzi, and they didn't ask any questions. As usual, Anzi's presence made everything okay, and if he wasn't saying anything, she saw no reason to mention their walkabout just to give her parents a chance to over react. She knew they wouldn't have approved of her exploring such remote and dangerous places, but she wondered if they had ever been to the bone temple, or even heard about the Bear or the thundering ear. It made her feel like it was all a dream, though. Getting no reaction from anyone made it seem as if nothing happened and nothing changed, despite how huge and important it all felt inside of her. Her mind quickly became numb with the pointless table chatter about weather and the productivity rate of different seed plantings. Her mind drifted far away until Mama brought up the weekend party plans, but only briefly. In turns, they each went off separately to fulfill the needs of the day.

Emilia felt like she was walking to school through a mist, cloaked by a veil. Like she was only a vague notion of her normal self. The complete lack of acknowledgment made her brain feel fuzzy. How could these two worlds exist side by side and not interact with each other? How could people not *know*? And if they *do* know, how could they not *care* and ask a million questions about it? And how could she still be just sitting here, now, knowing that there's something so much more, so much bigger and so incredibly full of power, history, and mystery? It was hard to imagine that just a few short days ago she was as oblivious as everyone else. She moved a bit more slowly today, lost in thought and not in such a hurry to be anywhere she had already been. Nothing ever changes.

"Everything okay?" Miguel's smile was a mix of enthusiasm and concern. "Why were you late to school? You're never late! And where were you yesterday?" He peppered her with questions, absentmindedly swinging his lunch bag, forgetting what it was for and that it was lunch time.

"You won't *believe* it, Miguel, come on!" she tugged his sleeve and he followed her to the farthest away picnic table.

"You're like, full of surprises, like every day! What's up?"

"Miguel, you *won't* believe this! Anzi took me for a hike yesterday! We were gone *all* day, 'til almost midnight! He just got up and announced we were going," she kept her voice low. "He showed me so many things! I can't talk about it now, it would take *way* too long. But it's *weird*, nobody said *anything*! My parents pretended like nothing happened. Doesn't *any*body want to know *any*thing around here?"

"They want to know when the movie theater's gonna get built..."

"Anything *important*!" she huffed and rolled her eyes at him, "I feel like I belong somewhere else. Or some*time* else."

"Like where? I mean... or when?"

"I don't know, but doing *this*," she flicked a dried up coffee bean off the table with her index finger, "is not it."

"Yeah, I know, nothing ever changes around here. I was thinking about what you said the other day, that we'll be planting and picking beans till we die here. When I really thought about it, it's the scariest thing I've ever heard!"

"It's *true*! I just don't know what to do about it."

"What about your grandfather? Did you tell him about what you saw?"

"Um, well, it didn't come up yesterday," a fact that surprised her now that she thought about it, "but I will soon."

"I hope I can get to know him better," Miguel's words made Emilia smile. Emilia's smile made Miguel's belly jumpy and his head a little woozy. He struggled for words from within the woozy. "Sooo, First Sat... I mean *Bella Luna* party at your place tomorrow!?"

"*Yes!!* I can't wait, and tomorrow's going to be a full moon, like it's supposed to be!"

"*That* will be cool!" said Miguel.

"I hope it's one of those nights when the old timers get into those little arguments they sometimes do. *That's* when the stories are best!" Emilia's voice held the whimsy of memory. She closed her eyes and inhaled deeply. "Sometimes their stories are so good, when I close my eyes I feel like I'm being transported back to those old days, like it's real!"

"It sounds like things were lots harder back then."

"Maybe," she pulled away from her inward gaze, back to Miguel to find his eyes locked with hers. "But there was so much, well, just so much more to be a part of, I think." Her mind overflowed with images of yesterday's journey. Despite her need to tell somebody, tell *everybody*, about her fantastical day, Emilia wasn't quite sure she was ready now that she had the chance. There was just too much to say and she still needed to process everything before sharing it. She resolved to choose her moment, but she was also about to burst, and so now became the moment.

"Miguel," Emilia reached across the table, put her hand on his arm and looked him straight in the eyes. "I *saw* the Bear! I saw *Calista!* For *real!*"

"What? What do you mean?"

"Good afternoon, class!" the teacher called from the top of the steps and students reluctantly found their way inside. The timing couldn't have been worse.

She might as well not have been in school at all. Emilia's mind was one hundred percent occupied with retracing all the steps she and Anzi made yesterday. She closed her eyes trying to recreate the feeling of seeing all the way to the bottom of the deep and wide ocean from high up on the cliff through Calista's eyes.

Down the hallway, Emilia saw Miguel walk through the door to the school yard. He couldn't see them coming up from behind, but she did, and quickened her pace. She was so done with bullies! They just didn't make sense to her. With all the things to do in this world, why would anyone choose to waste time being mean?

"Hey!" called Toro, tapping Miguel on the shoulder from behind, his cronies right beside him.

Miguel turned in the direction of the tap, but Toro was on his other side and blind-sided Miguel with a shove. Emilia jumped down the last two steps and landed next to Toro, fake-falling and slamming into his side, knocking him off balance and onto the ground.

"What is it with you? *Get off me!*" Toro exclaimed as he quickly stood up.

"Oh, sorry, Mr. Toro, sir. Please don't *punch* me," she taunted him.

"Outta my way, *Meely!*" he said.

Miguel stepped forward. Toro drew back to push him, but Emilia started talking fast.

"Why don't you guys pick on someone your own size and make some use out of yourselves!" she said.

"Why, little Meely-mouth is all like growing up and standing up for her *booyyfriend* again! Real brave of you!" Pug grimaced at Emilia.

Toro stared at Miguel, clenching his fists nervously at his sides. "Twerp!"

"Seriously," said Emilia firmly, holding her ground, "I have a job for you and your gang. Something nefarious–right up your alley."

All eyes were on her now.

"What's the deal? And since when are you *nefaarious*?" Toro mimicked to the laughter of his pals.

"I'll try to use *simple* words from now on," she rolled her eyes. With a sideways beckoning motion of her head, Emilia walked quickly away from the commotion of the doorway traffic with the curious gang close behind. Without warning, she turned around abruptly to face them. "You guys think you're pretty tough, but I'm not so sure. Here's your chance to prove it."

"What're you talking about? Ain't anybody here afraid of anything, except maybe your boyfriend, right fellas?" He pointed his thumb at Miguel but kept his suspicious eyes on Emilia.

"Yeah, that's right!" they all chimed in, trading brave looks, pushing and jabbing each other.

"Awright, whaddya got in mind, Miss *Nefaaarious*?" Toro lifted his chin at Emilia and rolled up his sleeves.

"Your family owns land in town right? At least they used to. Now it's Caláco's land. Same as my family," said Emilia.

"What of it?" Toro's eyes turned from suspicion to doubt.

"What if I told you they stole the land that someday would have been yours? They *stole* from you, Toro. Stole your future just like they stole mine. You want it back?"

"She's talking trash fellas, c'mon, let's roll." Toro rubbed his arms nervously and turned to walk.

"I have proof," Emilia stood steadfast.

Toro turned around. "What kinda proof?"

"I've seen it. You can see for yourself too. I'll tell you exactly where to go. Things are going to get worse around here, far worse. Unless you actually *like* having Caláco steal from you."

"It's true," said Miguel, moving next to Emilia. "I saw it too. They're getting close to doing something big. I dunno what, but it won't be a better world of anything for anyone."

"How bad do you want things to get before you do something? They'll take *everything* away from *all* of us." Emilia was stern, measured, and passionate. "Do *your* parents fight about it too?"

Toro's eyes darted nervously around his silent friends, who could only look blankly back at him and wait for his lead.

Emilia told them what she and Miguel saw from the mountain top. "You guys have a couple scooters between you, right? Go check it out for yourselves! I'll tell you exactly where to go. Tell me I'm wrong. I'd like to be."

"You better be right or I'll tell *you* exactly where to go! And I'll send you *both* there my*self*! Toro looked fiercely at Emilia, then at Miguel. "C'mon fellas." They turned and sauntered off, chattering among themselves.

"Em, that was brilliant!" exclaimed Miguel.

"I figured they were ready for a bigger challenge than us," said Emilia. "They just needed someone to steer them in a more interesting direction than beating people up."

"Maybe they'll find out something useful," said Miguel, "but," he hesitated, "I've never seen you act so, well, brave!"

"I've just had enough, Miguel! I'm sick of people thinking they can take advantage of me, or anyone they feel like, and get away with it! And to be honest? I'd rather get punched than live with not trying!"

"Well, it's worked pretty well for me," Miguel mused. He liked how it felt to hear Emilia laugh with him.

"Come on," said Emilia, "we should get to work."

"So, what do you mean you saw the Bear?" Miguel was antsy with restrained enthusiasm all afternoon.

There was finally a little time to recount some of the highlights of her day with Anzi. Walking through the woods to the ocean, down the cliff to the stone ear, the bone palace, and the mighty Bear skeleton. Miguel was enthralled at every word, eyes wide and mouth open in disbelief most of the time. She left a lot of details out, like Anzi's walking meditations, the scorpion bite, and "being the bear," because they were still too close to her nerves and she needed to sort out how she felt about these things before sharing. There wasn't nearly enough time to talk about the whirlwind into the past, which was just as well. As much as she wanted to tell him, the whole day seemed so fantastical, even to her, that he might think she was just making it all up. A slow drip of information she thought, rather than a gusher, might be best.

Emilia resented spending another tiny afternoon of her tiny life scratching the ground with her tiny tools, trying to make sense of the huge happenings all around her. Nobody saw the things she saw, and it was hard enough for her to believe them, why should anyone else? Yet, despite being unseen, they were all very, very real.

After an hour working under the hot sun, Emilia went to her pack to get a snack and some water. Miguel looked up and smiled at her, Emilia smiled back. In the distance, Papa wasn't smiling.

"Emilia!!" he called from across the field. "*Emilia!!*" He waved her over and she jogged to meet him.

"Yes, Papa?"

"Why don't you take the rest of the day off and go help your mother prepare for tomorrow."

Leaving those sad little beans behind made her incredibly happy, but then she thought of Miguel and wanted to be there for him, with him.

"Okay, thank you, Papa. I'll go get my things!" She took a couple of running steps, then turned back. "I'll see you this evening!" She pecked him on the cheek and ran off.

Papa spun around on one heel with his hand up, about to speak, but the words didn't arrive before her rapid departure. She ran back to where she had been working, stuffed the snacks into her bag, picked up her tools, and then sprinted to see Miguel, glancing over her shoulder as she did.

"What's up? You in trouble?"

"I'm going home to help get things ready for the party tomorrow. Are you doing anything tonight? Will you help me with the soup?"

"Sure."

She leaned toward his ear on her tiptoes, "You're awesome! Meet you at the bandstand after supper?"

"Sure." There wasn't any other answer Miguel ever had for Emilia. He agreed without hesitation, not knowing exactly what was happening at his own home tonight. He didn't always know how he would make things work out, but he usually found a way, especially if it meant being anywhere Emilia might be.

"Okay, see you later!"

"Sure. Later!" He shook his head fast from side to side to break the spell her breath had cast on him.

Emilia jogged out of the field, head down, not wanting to talk to anyone and already turning over the plans in her mind. She and Mama would prepare the main meal for tomorrow and others would bring a dish to share. It would be an incredible feast with endless food.

When she got home, Mama had just started preparing her special "push bread." Push bread was always delicious, always a little different from the last batch, and very fun to make and eat. And it was enormous. Beginning with a huge bowl of dough and a saved yeast starter, they folded into it different fruits, nuts, cheese, sometimes vegetables, and savory herbs. Then she added some bubbling, fermented agave juice that gave the sourdough a tangier bite and brought out the fruits' sweetness. The brick, stone, and clay oven, heated by a well-tended fire in the backyard, provided the ideal cooking environment. A good loaf (and it was *always* a good loaf) expanded so much while it cooked that it *pushed* the door of the oven open, hence its name. When that happened, the bread was done.

And of course there was the soup to build out. The first bowl was served, the story goes, at the very first Bella Luna celebration and at every one since. Nobody really knew exactly when that first day was, not even Anzi, but he remembered his grandparents talking about that ancient tradition. The soup was kept in a big barrel underground in the storage shed just outside of the park. Being underground kept it cool, but it also fermented over time, both of which helped to prevent it from spoiling. It was more than soup, but less than stew. It was reverently looked after by the entire village like a child whose parents were everyone. Throughout its history, the soup had been passed around, added to, shared when someone was unable to prepare their own food, and packed to nourish visiting travelers on their journey. The amount of soup ebbed and flowed over time, but the barrel never, *ever*, emptied. The flavor varied from year to year but a rich base of antiquity could always be tasted, and especially felt, just off the spoon.

As soon as she opened the front door, Emilia's sight fixed on the last of the roots and fruits from her now decimated garden waiting in a basket in the kitchen to be added to the soup. She hoped that nobody would ever add a single coffee bean to the soup, but it would soon be the only thing growing for miles around.

While Mama and Emilia worked on the soup and bread, and on tonight's meal, Papa and Anzi had come home and went about their own chores. They started by building a fire over the pit in the backyard for the pig roast, putting rocks on top of the wood so they got hot. Then they set up the tripod to hold the soup kettle over the fire, prepared the bread oven, set the lanterns, and generally cleaned things up. Once the pit fire was big enough, they knocked it down to where the rocks would hold the heat in the pit. Then they built up the fire again, and once it settled down to hot coals, they would drop an entire pig on top. The pig would be wrapped in large wet leaves so it wouldn't burn and then buried in more hot coals. The meat would slow roast underground until tomorrow. Anzi told her that cooking underground was a way of honoring the earth by giving back to it what it had given to them. She could taste the flavor of the ground in the food that grew from it and savored the smoky, succulent earthy flavor of food cooked within it.

They all sat down for dinner together and it was still as if everything that happened this week had never really happened. Despite the excitement of Bella Luna, every memory of her adventure with Anzi screamed loudly inside of her, but the slightest word of any of it would only invite conflict and surely ruin the entire weekend. Emilia struggled and just barely succeeded at putting the exhilarating secrets of her ancestral past aside so that she could enjoy the meal and a happy moment with her family. She wondered if Papa was thinking the same thing, or if he just didn't want to know at all. She glanced at him, then at Mama, chatting away. Still clueless. She imagined the warm resonance of the "scorpion bite" ebbing and flowing inside of her. She glanced at Anzi, who could only smile at her with a bright, but brief, sparkle. At least one person knew what she knew. She settled into their shared knowledge, and it was enough, at least for now. She needed this weekend to just have fun and do something a little bit less intense for a change.

After supper, Papa sat quietly and prepared his notes for the meeting, occasionally asking Anzi for his perspective. He spoke to him as a father trying to guide his son, rather than as the Senior Councilman trying to influence opinion. In his official role, Anzi held the duty to confer the Staff of Ceremony to the host, giving the bearer certain authority. As host, Papa would speak first, and this responsibility was an honor he took seriously. He knew that because of his position in the community, his words would be considered by discerning ears and in turn, reflect back on his role as field supervisor for Caláco. Emilia did not envy his position of having to try and please everyone, but he seemed to be good at it, at least most of the time, as long as she didn't count herself as part of 'everyone.'

"Mama, I'm going to get the soup now." Emilia brought her plate to the sink.

"Do you need help?" her mother asked.

"No, I can manage."

"Are you sure? It can be hard to keep that rickety old cart steady, and it will be dark soon!"

"I'll be fine."

"Maybe I should come with you, let me just wash my hands."

"No, really, Mama, I'll be fine!"

Mama looked at her with that sidelong look mothers have, that question they ask using only the expression on their face that says, *oh, really, and just how exactly does that work?* The truth was never far behind that look.

"I, well, Miguel will help me. He's going to meet me there so you don't need to worry about it!"

Mama's face relaxed and softened. She liked Miguel, and held the long family friendship close. "Go on then, and hurry back, there's lots to do!" she said, turning quickly back to her work so as not to reveal the smile on her face that might embarrass her daughter.

Emilia grabbed the cart from the back of the house, piled buckets and lids into it, and jogged off into the warm spring evening, pushing the cart always to the left to keep it going straight. She had a smile on her face and in her heart.

Miguel sat on the bandstand swinging his legs waiting for Emilia. He saw her wheel the cart into the park and sprang up, beating out a rhythm on the handrail with his hands as he leapt over it with a whoop, hands in the air and landing like an Olympic gymnast for the prize.

"Sorry to keep you waiting, Miguel!" she called, laughing at his antics as she and the cart bounced to a stop just in front of him. "There's so much to do at home," she panted after running most of the way, "and this stupid cart just goes wherever it wants!"

"It's okay, I just got here a minute ago." He had in fact been there for over half an hour. Anticipation did not allow him to sit still at home and he didn't want to chance keeping her waiting.

"Did you check out the shed yet?" she asked as she sat to rest on the bandstand.

"No, thought I'd wait for you." He sat down next to her. "I haven't been to the soup shed in so long, I almost forgot it was there!" He was still doing gymnastics on his insides and found it impossible to sit still. He jumped up and examined the cart, fussing with the wheels.

Emilia slid off the bandstand. "Come on!"

Miguel took the cart by its handles and they walked to the edge of the park where the leafy green canopy shadowed the waning sunlight. The overgrown path revealed its outline in the dusk. Miguel cleared some brush with his foot, tugged the cart over broken branches, then turned and held out his hand for Emilia. She took it, only pretending to need it to balance her step. They continued walking slowly, dividing their hands between each other and the cart handles. The dimming path quickly brought them to their destination.

The shed showed its age and was in need of attention. It served as a community root cellar and storage for some old equipment used for planting, harvesting, and processing grains and corn. And of course the soup, which found a secure home inside and underground since forever. Without thinking about it, they stopped simultaneously and stood quietly for a moment in front of the shed, taking in a tangible reverence that seemed to wrap around it in the twilight. Emilia imagined the steps and voices of everyone who had ever walked this path for who knows how long, then smacked her lips as if she could already taste the soup.

She squeezed Miguel's hand, their heads turned and eyes locked. Between them, they suddenly became the north and south poles of a magnet, and the pull could not be stopped. A surge of energy flowed through their fingertips and through their lips and tongues. She pulled her head back and looked hard into his eyes, searching. He looked back, squinting as if a bright light had just blinded him.

"Woaa!" he exclaimed.

She buried her face in his neck, not wanting to talk about the spark she was sure he saw in her eyes, but happy he could see it. She just wanted to enjoy an uncomplicated and very real moment.

Then, opening her eyes, looking over his shoulder she saw it, not too far away in the fading light. A fallen tree. And another, and another. She gasped and pulled away from Miguel.

"I know, fireworks, right?" said Miguel, dreamily.

"*Look!*" Emilia exclaimed.

"What?"

"Over there, don't you see it?" She grabbed his hand, turned him around, and pulled him down the path a bit more. They stared at the damage. At least a dozen trees were all cut down with a chainsaw.

"See?!" said Emilia. "They're coming! They're coming for *everything*!"

Their playground for as long as they could both remember was in jeopardy.

"*No!*" gasped Miguel. "Is this what you saw when you followed the roar?"

"Yes, only it was much, *much* worse. Where will they *stop*?"

"I don't know, but they can't take over the park! They wouldn't do that, would they?"

"Look, Miguel, they *are* doing it! I don't think there's *anything* they wouldn't do if they thought it could make them money! UNNG!" Emilia stamped her feet on the ground.

"How do we stop them?"

"How can we? Everybody wants *progress*! I *hate* progress if this is what it means!"

"Em, there's nothing we can do about it now. Maybe it's just maintenance or something. Let's get the soup and get back to your place before it gets too late. We can ask your parents. I'm sure *somebody* knows about it."

"Okay. Let's get the soup and get out of here," Emilia agreed.

The shed was never locked, but merely secured to keep animals out. Miguel poked at the tilting shed door hanging from a single hinge.

"What do you think happened?" asked Miguel.

"Looks like an animal got in!" said Emilia.

"It would have to be a mighty big animal, like a bear!" said Miguel, causing Emilia to flinch at the accusation against bears in general.

"Or a human. *Look!*" She pointed to the ground where boot prints made a clear impression in the soil. "Oh, no. No, no NO!"

"*Not the soup!*" they both cried out at once.

It took both of them to hold up the door so it wouldn't fall off the remaining hinge as they slowly pushed it open. The shelves had been rummaged and left in disarray, canning jars smashed on the floor, fermenting vegetables spilled out, and old wooden barrels overturned.

"Why would anyone *do* this? Everyone knows they can take whatever they need!" exclaimed Emilia.

"Maybe they thought there was booze in the barrels!" said Miguel.

"It was *them*, I *know* it! Caláco-loco and their thieves!"

"But why?" asked Miguel.

"They probably want to clear everything and plant coffee here too!" Emilia muttered, bending down to lift the top off a wooden bench. Under the bench was a hatch in the floor leading to where the soup was kept. She opened the hatch, got on her knees, and peered into the dark hole.

"It's okay! They didn't get into it!" Emilia was relieved. To her, the soup was living history, a connection to everything that ever made her and the village what they are. Losing the soup would be like losing her entire heritage. Her grandmother helped make the soup at some point, and it would be like losing part of her family. "Help me get it into those buckets, Miguel."

Miguel held her hand as Emilia jumped down into the pit.

After she landed, she looked up at him, smiling, her arm stretched almost to its limit. "Um, Miguel?"

"What?"

"You can let go now."

"Oh! Yeah, uh, right. Sorry." He let go immediately, wiped the sweat from his hand, jumped up and grabbed the buckets from the cart. "Here," he said, handing them and a flashlight down to her.

She knelt down and opened the spigot on the bottom of the barrel. The smell of old wood and dirt mixed with the tangy, fruity, earthy aromas of the soup as it glugged out into the first bucket. She closed her eyes, inhaled deeply, and the room filled with visions and memories, some of them hers, others unknown.

She handed each filled bucket up to Miguel, who kept busy trying to repair the damaged shed and secure the door. With the last bucket lifted, he delivered his hand down to hers and though not in need of it, she was happy for his steadying influence on the rickety wooden ladder. The cart was full almost to breaking and they secured the shed door as best they could.

"C'mon Emilia, we need to go tell our parents about this!"

"No!" Emilia was more abrupt than she intended. "I don't think we should. My father will go crazy! He's already stressed out enough about tomorrow!"

"Seriously?"

"Promise me!" implored Emilia.

"Okay, it's not like anything's going to happen overnight, and we can't do anything about it till tomorrow anyway."

"I need to know if you're with me on this. I mean *really* with me," she looked him dead square in the eyes. "We need to get to the bottom of it, get answers, and make them stop! But our timing has to be right."

"Of course! I don't like it any more than you do. Why so intense?"

"Just trust me, Miguel, okay?" She took both of his hands in hers, "We can't tell *anyone* until tomorrow, until the meeting, until the time is right!"

"Plan. Now let's get this soup back to your place," Miguel complied.

And off they rolled, each with a handle in their hands, weaving, wondering, and laughing, taking their time getting home.

It was dark when they got back to Emilia's house. They went straight to the backyard, splattered with low moonlight and dim light from inside the house, poured the soup into the giant cauldron hanging over the fire pit, and covered it. Emilia went inside to the kitchen where Mama was cleaning up.

"Did you get the soup alright?"

"Yes, Mama. We just poured it into the cauldron. Miguel is lighting the fire."

"Very good. Would you please take those and add them to the soup?" she motioned to the baskets of food on the counter that neighbors brought for the soup. "And just a small fire for the night so the soup doesn't heat past a slow simmer. Oh, and check the coals over the pit too, okay? Papa will check it again later."

"Of course, Mama."

"Thank you, mija, I think most everything we can do tonight is done." She sat down with a heave and a sigh, kicked off her shoes, leaned her head back, closed her eyes, and rubbed her feet. "I'm going to bed soon. Don't stay up too late; we'll both need to get up early."

"Okay, Mama, don't worry, I'll take care of everything. See you in the morning."

"And don't disturb your father; he's working on his talk for tomorrow."

"Okay, good night, Mama!"

She was happy that Papa was busy, and Anzi was probably already in bed, a happy set of circumstances that offered some quiet time with Miguel. Thrilled to have a bigger part in the preparation this year, she brought the baskets outside where they stirred each fruit, vegetable, and spice into the soup, recounting stories from the day, memories of past Bella Luna gatherings, and considered how they would bring up the destruction of the shed and the trees in the park. They didn't come up with any good way to do it, so decided to leave it in the hands of tomorrow, trusting that the right moment would arrive and at least one of them would recognize it when it did.

"Miguel, do you believe in magic?"

"There's always a trick to magic, it's just a matter of whether you're paying attention or not. It's not real, magic is just an illusion."

"Not that kind of magic, I mean *real* magic, the kind you can feel and know it's true even if you don't understand it."

Miguel's belly was churning again. "Liiiike..." He almost said out loud, *Like how it feels to hold your hand?* but he chickened out, and mumbled instead, "Like, what do you mean?"

"Like my grandfather's eyes. Did you ever notice..." She didn't know how to finish.

"Yeah, they kind of wander and have a shimmery look sometimes, it makes me want to stare at him when I see it, but that just feels weird, and I don't want to be rude."

"Right, but I think there's more, though. Do you?"

"You mean more about your grandfather's eye thing? What do you mean?" Miguel wanted to be honest, but given his innate ability to say the wrong thing, he didn't want to chance it.

"I don't know, I just feel like there's more to life than what we think it is, more than just all the stuff we do every day." She didn't know what else to say or how to say it without sounding confusing or crazy.

"Sometimes," he hesitated, staring into the fire, "well, sometimes I feel like things just work out for me. Like I'm just in the right place at the right time. Sometimes I get punched in the nose, but then sometimes I get a kiss." He looked at the ground feeling heat build in his face and hoped that the light of the fire masked his blushing. Emilia smiled and he continued. "It's like I know, like I can feel when I'll be okay even if things look bad. I try not to think about it too much, but sometimes I wonder if it's my mom, you know, from the other side, kind of, you know, looking out for me."

Emilia took his hand and they both just stood and stared into the fire. Soon it was roaring and hot enough that it could be knocked down to coals and the soup would simmer safely until morning.

"I have to get my bike from the park and get home, Em. I'm really glad we got to do this together."

"Me too." She lifted his hands, then lifted herself on her toes, and kissed him once on the lips. "See you tomorrow!"

"Tomorrow!" Miguel grinned widely and clapped his hands. "Tomorrow!" he said again with a swivel in his hips, punching the sky with his hands.

"Tomorrow!" Emilia smiled and curtsied dramatically as he turned and jogged off.

She stood alone under the stars by the hot coals and leaned in over the soup steam while giving it a stir. The smell lured her into one last taste before covering it to simmer overnight. Closing her eyes, the flavors swirled around her mouth and she imagined the first soup being made so long ago. The taste of history spread its texture across her tongue, funneled through time directly into her belly to be absorbed into her core and become part of her being. She had the odd feeling that she was growing very large on the inside: wider, taller, steadier. She felt as though she were enveloped in a cozy skin of soft, thick, protecting fur, and imagined being with Calista and seeing through her eyes again. She saw the bulldozers, the soup shed, the bone temple, the ocean depths, and her garden. She saw everything all at once. It made her feel tall and full, and the fullness engulfed her even more. Silently, inwardly, she asked Calista what she wanted from her.

Anzi's quiet voice rode the evening air through the open window to the outside where it struck her ears and jarred her back to here and now. She pulled the spoon from her mouth at the same moment Anzi's words pulled the heat from her body. She stood frozen, listening to the intense discussion that was escalating inside the house.

"I am not happy about this future you have chosen. But I am an old man and have lived my life. You and your daughter will need to spend your lives in the future you are creating today. I can only advise you that the goals and money you seek will not last and are not the most important things."

"You don't under*stand*, Father. This *is* our future and it's time to let go of the past." Papa sounded so sure and confident. "Don't you see that this is the progress that will bring us all into the larger world we want to be part of! I need to do this for my family, and for all the families in the village, just as you did when you signed the original agreement. You knew then, as I do now, that the ways of the past, the ways that worked for you as a young man, don't work for us anymore."

Anzi's voice carried both strength and patience. "There is much time between then and now, and many lessons learned from experience. You are still a young man, but the past is what carried you to today. You have been riding atop its shoulders without ever looking to see what is beneath you, *or* behind you. Those things you can know if you only look. What you think you see ahead of you is obscured by blinders and amounts to little more than fantasy. The only thing you can know for sure about your future is that it is built upon this moment."

"You know I don't disrespect our history or our family, but the past must step aside for the future, and the future means *progress!* I cannot live in your past, Father! *We* cannot live there. That time was yours. Today is very different. Tomorrow we will decide." His voice lifted and slowed, "I think we both know how it will be."

"You know that your daughter is not the only one who feels as she does. And *she* will be the future one day. You must think of her, her generation, and those many to come!"

"My daughter is *always* the first thing on my mind! As a parent, you know that!" His voice lowered, "Or perhaps you don't."

Anzi scowled, "Yes, I was an impetuous young man. Driven, as you are. I am not proud of everything I have done, and *you* know that *very* well, my son. I have made my amends and set my path straight.

"I'm sorry, Father. Yes, I do know that. Forgive me, I am very tired. But I *know* that *this* is the right path for us!" Ernesto emphasized each word with a thump of his hand on the desk.

"It seems people do not learn *from* other's mistakes, they learn to *make* those same mistakes all over again on their own! I do not know how humanity survives like this!" Anzi sounded weary.

Emilia watched in silence at the animated shadow figures playing themselves out through the window.

"This is a difficult time and we both know that," Ernesto continued. "I will deliver my views in the most positive light. My message will embrace progress and collaboration while putting those opposed at ease. But listen to me: we *all* have too much invested in coffee and Caláco now to go give up and go backward!"

"You will deliver your message and it will be heard. But take great care in what you are asking of the past. To see its way through to your future, the plan must be managed well." With a sigh Anzi added, "And I do not see that that has happened thus far. There has only been the disappearing of us."

"Please, Father, not *now*! Please don't start with your fantasies of the old days! They are stories. Myths of your imagination! They are *not real!*"

"Do you presume that the air is clear because you believe that you can see through it?" asked Anzi in a quiet voice.

And then there was only one shadow.

10 - CALÁCO

Tree tops and stumps lay strewn and scattered in the clearing while men and machines attempted to order the chaos by pushing, pulling, dragging, digging, stacking, and burning. The ground was wetter now compared to when it supported the dense forest. Rivulets of water coursed through a mosaic of muddy hummocks. The soft soil caused the left side of the well-used mobile office trailer to sink into the ground at the edge of the clearing, stretching and bending the siding and pulling at window frames. Dirt and dust kicked up by machines and splattered by rain stuck to the neglected walls of the Caláco Corporation's headquarters.

Inside the trailer, litter from coffee cups, food packaging, and paperwork radiated disarray outward from the desk and chair at the sunken end. This was a temporary situation during the planning phase for construction of the industrial infrastructure that would one day be a global destination consisting of the coffee plantation, corporate offices, and tourist theme park.

The stains he wore on his shirt blended in well with the clutter. A notebook rested on the desktop nameplate *G. Bigly, III.* He completely filled the chair he sat in all day, every day, shuffling papers, swearing at his computer, and arguing on the phone. Exactly on schedule, his site manager, Mr. Tode, arrived for the daily briefing.

"They aren't working tomorrow? And they just told you this now?" growled Bigly, looking up through a furry raised unibrow that stretched over both of his eyes. "And you're okay with that...?"

"Yessir, I mean, no sir, I'm not okay with it. But they have a holiday. Some pagan tradition they seem to think is important. Some of them even left early today."

"And you just let them have this unannounced holiday?" One side of Bigly's eyebrow drooped, the other raised in suspicion.

"Well, I... there were enough of them talking about it... that..."

"I see. You thought to keep them placated, make them feel some hope?"

"Yessir! They work harder when there's something to look forward to."

"And this involves the entire village, you say?"

"Yessir, everyone," Tode dragged on his cigarette, using it to light another, then reached over the desk and handed it to Bigly.

"Good. Good." he twisted his hands and accepted Tode's offer. "We can make this work for us. Perhaps even get a bit ahead of schedule."

"Our core teams have moved to area four, sir. And the new team has already been deployed. If we focus our efforts, construction will begin by early summer."

"That is a schedule that will *need* to be kept, *Tode!*" The cigarette dangled from his mouth and danced with his words as he half-stood from his chair, squinting at Tode to make his point. "That extra team you recommended has put us *over* budget. Our investors are *not* happy. It took me *years* to secure the financing to make *my* dream, my father's *and* my grandfather's dream, a reality!" He leaned forward on his desk, exhaling smoke dramatically before standing completely up, a process that, for him, took a bit more than the usual amount of effort. He continued in a more forceful tone, "There's no more credit, the interest continues to mount, and our stock price is plummeting! If this poor planning doesn't end *now*, *more* heads will roll!" He banged on the desk with his clenched fist causing everything on it to shake and squinted into Tode's rabbit-like eyes. "Don't disappoint me, Tode. Don't disappoint my grandfather!" He snuffed out the cigarette in the overfilled ashtray.

Tode shifted, looked away, swallowed hard, then looked back. "Yessir. Understood, sir! I assure you, sir,that we *will* be ahead of schedule inside of two months. You'll see! And with the proper news spin, the stock price will rebound, then we'll increase the profit margin as we discussed with the executive team! The cash will start flowing soon!"

"Let's hope you can keep that promise, Tode," he said now in a more measured tone, sitting down again with a heave. "There will be no more delays and no more days off! Not for you and not for the laborers!"

"Yessir. Understood, Mr. Bigly, sir!"

"Now, let's take advantage of their distraction. Let them have their little party. Move the new team to the park. That ground is fertile and will yield well. Once they've had enough drink they won't even notice."

"Yessir, we've already begun clearing trails there. We'll proceed with the clear-cut tomorrow, *ahead of schedule*! Good plan, sir!"

"And take down that dilapidated old shack! I'll have my personal office built there. This crooked trailer is making me sick. I deserve better!" Bigly swiveled his chair so that his back was facing Tode and he stared out the window, satisfied with the progress represented by the desolate scene outside. A faint grin coiled up under the beads of sweat on his upper lip.

"Yessir. Understood, sir!" Tode turned and stumbled down the crooked steps of the crooked trailer, fumbling nervously for another cigarette. He took a few minutes outside to survey the work being done and consider his approach. With the nerve and resolve of abundant nicotine coursing through his blood, he got on the phone and gave the crew leaders their new orders. It did not go well; it would take some time to move equipment around, redeploy personnel, and get set up again. With the schedule demands, it would mean working a second or even third shift into the night. Nobody was happy about it. Copious threats and curses were exchanged. Tode reassured himself of having the higher moral ground because he offered work and pay for the large crew. And yet the workers continued to complain, something he did not understand, and that made him worry for his own job.

For him, the docile and subservient village laborers were much easier to handle than the seasoned and surly work crews. Bigly and Tode made sure to keep the village Council on a slow-drip feed, sharing only the minimum amount of information. Manipulation was an art mastered by Caláco management, and the key to their success. The pride that the village community had in their own honesty and perseverance served Caláco's tactics well. Tode knew he had the upper hand; the villagers had no idea about the full scope of their plans. He needed only one more cover story before he and his teams moved in for the next appropriation. He would need to invent that story before tomorrow's inevitable outcry over their confiscated park. If they didn't like his story, all he had to do was show them the contract they signed and threaten their jobs. They had nothing else, and so everything, to lose.

The next phone call he made was to his wife, at home far away.

"How are you feeling? ... And what did the Doctor say? ... Oh, that's good news! Have you been getting the checks I send? ... Good, yes, that's all of them ... Well, I'm afraid I'll need to stay a while longer than expected... No, it's not like that! Please believe me, it's all work all the time, and Bigly ... Yes, I know ... Yes, I remember that conversation ... Yes, you were right. And the children? ... I miss them terribly, and you! I can't wait to get out of here and get home ... I know, I'm sorry, dear, but we need the money, and the bonus should be substantial if I can keep to the current schedule ... Yes, of course I love you. Hug the children for me."

He held the phone to his ear until there was silence. Desperation clenched tightly around his heart.

Their scooters buzzed along the wooded trail until the tree canopy started to open up and the trail became more worn and muddy. They stopped and put their bikes down, then walked ahead until they could get a view through the trees.

"Looks like Meely-mouth was right for a change," Toro said as the boys surveyed the clear-cut from a safe distance.

"Wow! That thing is huge!" exclaimed, Pug. "It's kind of cool what you can do with these big machines. Maybe I can get a job driving it!"

Toro punched him in the arm. "Shut up! My grandparents told me stories about some old stuff hidden around here. It might be worth something! They'll just wreck it or keep it for themselves!" He paused and continued to watch the machines. "They are kinda cool, though."

"So, what're we gonna do?" asked Pug.

"Well, if Meely's right, they're about to move into the village. And from what I saw on my way through the park today, they'll be starting there, and then who knows."

"They're gonna wreck the park!?" said Pug incredulously.

"If anybody's gonna wreck this place it'll be *us*, not *them*!" said Toro, his anger rising at the prospect of someone stealing something he could make better use of by stealing it himself.

"Yeah, that's right! This is *our* place, not *theirs*!" Pug punched his open palm as he said it.

The other boys chimed in with agreement, "Who told them they could be here anyway?"

"Right! Let's take 'em down, guys!"

"Yeah, take 'em out! How're we gonna do that, T?" They all looked inquisitively at Toro.

"First," Toro took control, "everybody swears to *total* secrecy. Stealth mode on! Agreed?" He looked them each in the eye.

"Agreed!" the others said, nearly in unison. They stood in a circle and each one made a fist with their right hand, thrusting it in front of them into the center of the circle. When all their fists bumped, they let out a single, simultaneous, "HOOT!" to signal their solidarity to each other.

"Awright, who's got candy? C'mon, I know you all scored something at school today! Show!"

They all dug into their pockets and pulled out an assortment of pocket lint, appropriated coins, and candies.

"What the hell is that?" Toro looked at the small woven fuzzball figure in one boy's hand.

"Mine! Good luck charm," he stuffed it back in his pocket. "My gram gave it to me."

"Whatever," said Toro, shaking his head. "Listen up, here's the plan. They've probably got more of those tree machine things in the garage over there. We come in from the back corner, there," he pointed, "and slide down low across the wall to the front doors. They won't be able to see us from where they're working."

Pug was looking off in the distance. "What about that guy standing outside the trailer?"

Toro squinted in the direction Pug was looking. "He's on the phone. He won't see us," he assured them. "When we get inside, drop the candy into the gas tanks. It'll dissolve and the sugar will gum up the fuel. They'll never know."

"Brilliant! How'd you figure that out?" Pug obliged with a compliment.

"Accident. Spit out a gross sugar-bomb once and it landed in a bucket of gas from a scooter I was working on. Thing kept stalling out till I cleaned the tank and found what was left of it."

The boys all laughed. They were getting antsy and a little nervous.

"Hold out your hands," said Toro.

The boys obeyed and Toro pulled more candies out of his own pockets and divvied them up. "Use 'em all!" he commanded as the boys stuffed their pockets.

Pug kept glancing over his shoulder. "I still don't like the looks of that guy."

"Just stay low. Stealth – on!" Toro whispered sternly, squatted, picked up some dirt in his hands and rubbed it on his face. The others followed his lead. He pointed with two fingers first at his eyes, then at the target garage, and started jogging in a half-squatted position, the others in close formation. They regrouped at the edge of the woods just behind the garage. Toro put a finger to his lips and pointed to the large door where they would go in. Crouching down, they ran as quietly as they could along the outside wall and ducked into the large, open bay door. The machines towered over them. Toro ran to the back and took cover behind one of the giant tires, joined quickly by the others. There were three machines in the garage, and one car.

"Pug, you take this one, you guys take the other one, I'll get the last," Toro ordered. "Look for the gas cap!"

They climbed up and around the machines like they were giant jungle gyms.

"Found it!" Pug shouted.

"Shhhhh! Dump the candy in!" Toro whispered loudly.

The boys couldn't resist sitting in the cab and playing with the levers, while Toro jumped off the machine he just monkey-wrenched and put the rest of his candy into the car's gas tank for good measure. It was a beautiful car. Sleek, shiny, long, and black, with lots of chrome. He took a brief moment to admire how the tree machines could easily roll over the car, leaving nothing but a pancake of metal behind. The potential for destruction was difficult for him to walk away from.

They completed their task and regrouped again by the garage door under cover of a giant spare tire lying on the floor. Toro jabbed his fist forward, the others did the same and mouthed a silent, "Hoot!" Toro stood first and before the others could stand, he was squatting back down.

He put one finger over his mouth and held his other hand up to his ear as if talking on a phone. He pointed in the direction he saw Tode walking from. Using hand signals, he motioned for the others to move to the back of the garage. Ducking as low as they could, they moved fast in a single file. Pug saw it first, pointing to a small door in the wall on the other side of the garage. They all ran for it and didn't stop until they made it to the scooters. The last boy tripped over a tool lying on the floor and it banged into the wall with a loud, echoing clang. He fell and rolled out the door, limp-running to catch up.

"Who's there?!" shouted Tode, just coming in through the big bay doors. There was nothing but silence. He walked to where he heard the noise. "Hey!" he shouted into the cavernous building. Nothing but an echo.

When he got to the back of the garage Tode saw the open door and ran over to it. Through the woods he saw a dust cloud and heard the distant buzz of scooters. He could see that the last boy was obviously injured because he was still running with a limp. Tode ran after him, but after a few steps, realized the futility of chasing them on foot. He got into the car, put his hand on the key, then thought Bigly would never forgive him if he put even a scratch on it. Tode reached for his phone and keyed in his boss's number. He hesitated before hitting the talk button, staring at the numbers and running the scenario through his head. The last thing he needed now was more trouble. He looked around and didn't see anything missing. He pushed the power off button and put the phone back in his pocket. "Kids," he muttered.

11 – PREPARATION

Emilia tossed and turned, endlessly replaying every minute of the last few days. There was almost too much to think and feel, and all of it new. She tried to put everything into the greater context of her life but couldn't see how to fit the pieces together. She felt like a magnet for crazy, intense things. Sleep, Anzi told her, is the only way to access the gift of dreams, and that there are forces at play that do not want you to receive those gifts. She tried as best she could to hold on to her dreams during the day, but it seemed an impossible task sometimes and lately, her dreams only added to her confusion. Between frustration, exhaustion, and willpower, she managed to put all the confusion aside, close her eyes, and focus on the one thing she knew she needed now. She learned somewhere, maybe from Anzi or maybe from another dream, that humming a single, steady note in her head and placing it gently between her eyes helped to mask the noise of the day and allow solace to overtake commotion. It wasn't easy, but it worked every time to provide a focus that cut through the distraction of random thoughts. Soon the trick worked and she slept hard.

The huge white skeleton stood tall on hind legs, jaws open wide as if to roar, but no sound accompanied the action. She shook her head and landed with a tremendous, bony clatter when her front feet hit the ground. It was a fearsome sight, but there was no power in it because there was no will of the flesh to hold the spirit. Calista rattled toward Emilia and as she did, her clattering gait resolved to an elegant gallop. Flesh and fur covered the bear, restoring her to her grandeur. Emilia moved steadily forward, fearlessly, faster. Neither one stopped until they were merged, feeling the other's feelings, thinking the other's thoughts until there was no distinction between the bony bear and the furry girl. She awoke with a shot and sat up straight with her eyes wide open, the dream still moving through her.

"EMILIA!!" The urgency of her mother's voice heaved her tired body from bed.

How could it be morning already? It felt like only minutes since she went to bed. She shook off sleep enough for a groggy reply, "Coming!" The sun was already high in the sky. She didn't know why, but Mama had let her sleep in.

Today would be a whirlwind, starting this very second. There was still lots to do and no time to think about anything. She sat in bed for a short moment, rubbed her eyes, stretched, and then got up and dressed. She walked past the washroom where Papa and Anzi were giving themselves a hot milk-shave with single long-bladed razors and shaving paste made from goat's milk.

"Good morning, young lady!" Anzi glanced at Emilia, still holding the razor blade, and winked. Then he patted and pinched Papa's cheeks saying, "Soft as a baby's bottom!" and they all three burst out laughing. She was glad that they seemed to have put aside their differences, at least for the time being. She wanted this day to be special, but the possibility for uncontrolled release of tension was high, and disaster would be the only outcome.

In the kitchen, Emilia took her place amid the frenzy of cooking, eating, cleaning, and generally running around getting things done. Mama was putting together some simple appetizers. "Have yourself some breakfast and go check on the soup, okay? Oh, and the bread is in the oven, help me keep an eye on it!"

Emilia cut up some fruit and cheese and took her plate outside where she could escape the frenzy and ease into the morning. She stoked the fire, stirred the soup, and checked on the bread by cracking open the oven door and peeking inside. It was a huge mass of golden dough, browning and growing, but not yet ready. She busied herself with tidying up and decorating when Papa and Anzi came outside briefly to stoke the fire on top of the pit.

"Spectacular!" said Anzi, beaming.

Papa was being very businesslike and hurried around checking on things. "Good, all very good! I need to find more chairs. Do you think there are enough lights for tonight?"

"I was thinking just one more string of the colored lights between the house and the big tree." Emilia had the scene planned out in her head. "I'll go get them."

"Excellent," said Papa and very quickly he was back in his office.

When Emilia came back with the lights, she could hear the faint crackling of Anzi's radio through the window. Mama was still working in the kitchen.

The brakes on Miguel's bicycle screeched loudly as he rolled up to the edge of the yard and jumped off while it was still moving. "How's it going, Em?"

"Oh, hey, Miguel!" She spun half way around on a single heel to greet him.

Miguel looked up from the dust raised at her feet and into her eyes. "You move like a flower in the breeze!" he said quietly, and then instantly averted his eyes, swinging his arms uncomfortably. "Uhhh... I mean... you ready for today?"

She blushed a little and was glad to see him, but felt the usual mix of calm and turmoil in his presence. "I guess, I mean, I guess I... don't really know. It's kind of crazy inside." She wanted to tell someone about her dream, she wanted to tell Anzi, but there wouldn't be any time for that today. She wanted to tell Miguel, but everyday things piled up inside of her and the story only got longer and more complicated.

"Well, let me know if you need any help. I need to ride around for a while, just to get out; you know." Miguel sensed awkwardness but couldn't tell if it came from him or her or if it was all his imagination. He picked up his bike and straddled it, then asked, "How's the soup looking?"

"Come on, let's try it!" He jumped off his bike again and she led him by the hand to the giant kettle with a bounce in her step. She took off the lid and they both leaned in over the steam, simultaneously inhaling with a harmonious and enthusiastic, "*mmmm*". Taking the spoon off the hook where it hung, Emilia dipped some soup into it, blew over it, and held it to Miguel's mouth. He gently slurped the hot, spicy brew over his lips.

"Unbeli*eee*vable!" he pronounced. "That's the most delicious thing I've ever tasted!"

Emilia took what was left in the big spoon and slurped it down. She closed her eyes and swirled it in her mouth. "MMMMM!!!! Oh, that is *sooo* good! Can you taste it, Miguel? Can you taste the old days? Can you taste the last of my garden?" She stamped her feet with excitement. "MMMmmm!"

"I *can* taste it, Emilia. And I want more!" He followed the words borne from his mouth until his lips landed on Emilia's, where they lingered for somewhere between a few seconds and eternity.

"Delicious!" they said simultaneously and burst out laughing long and loud, eventually landing on the garden bench.

Emilia couldn't sit still for more than a few seconds. "Help me put up this string of lights."

They worked together tying the lights up around most of the perimeter of where they thought people would be when it got dark, then stood back to look them over.

"AH! Miguel!" she jumped up and over to the bread oven in a single springboard leap. "The bread, help me with the bread!" The oven doors were pushed wide open by the expanded, well-baked dough.

"How do you get it out?"

"From the top. Grab the two poles sticking out of that side," she directed.

They both squatted to get under the log handles on each side of the oven and lifted until the top came off. The heavy adobe forced grunts out of each of them. The top came up and pulled at the bread as they lifted, stretching it until it dropped back down to the hearth. They slid the top sideways onto a wooden support, leaving the top half of the bread exposed.

"Now open the doors..." she said as she was doing so. "Get those paddles!" She pointed to the two long-handled bread paddles leaning against the house. "You go in from that side. Pull the hatch out." Miguel was quick with the paddles and they each slid one under the giant loaf.

"Careful, *caaarefull*!" they traded the word as they lifted, wiggled, and coerced the bread until it was loose from the sides, then lifted it up and over the oven side wall. It was heavy. *Really* heavy. And in their excitement they had forgotten to position the table to put it on.

"Over there!" Emilia pointed with her nose to the table.

Their arms see-sawed under the weight of the bread balanced on the paddles.

"Ooh, no, nononono! Catch it!" she cried as the bread tilted unexpectedly toward the ground.

"Got it! Steadyyyy..." said Miguel.

Each time it rocked to one side they were able to compensate just in time before the whole thing crashed to the ground. Arms and knees buckling under the strain, the bread got lower and lower as they walked and balanced. With one last coordinated lift they hefted the enormous and perfectly baked loaf up and onto the table where it would remain until it was no more. They both collapsed on the ground out of breath.

"I thought we'd lose it!" gasped Miguel. "That was *heavy*!" He sat up straight. "I can't wait to try it!"

"There was *no – way* we were going to lose it!" She looked him directly in the eye. "Miguel, I'm really glad you stopped by. But there's so much I have to do. We can talk later, okay?"

"You're beautiful," Miguel said without hesitation, picking up her hand and putting it in his, "and today is already incredible! Are you ready?"

"Yes, I'm ready, of course I'm ready!" she smiled and laughed lightly as they helped each other up.

Miguel looked down at the ground, then back up into her eyes, and leaned in with a big hug.

Emilia whispered into his ear, "I'll see you later." She turned to stir the soup and Miguel stoked the fire with a few logs.

"Okay," said Miguel, heading for his bike, "I will see you soon, my flower in the breeze!"

"Don't be late!" she called after him with a huge smile and a laugh.

"I will never be late!" he called back, already rolling. "MY BEAUTIFUL FLOWER WHO DANCES WITH THE BREEZE!" His voice trailed off as he spun out of sight down the road. She couldn't see it, but Miguel punched the sky with both hands.

"Everything all right out here?" Mama called from the doorway. "What was all that commotion?"

"Oh, Miguel. He just stopped by to see if he could help. We got the bread out; it looks perfect!"

"Very good! Much to do now, I could use your help in here if you're done outside."

"Okay, Mama, everything looks good, and the soup is *incredible* this year!"

"Of course it is! Were you expecting something less?"

"No, *really*, it really is *way* better than I remember it, *ever*!"

"Many spices flavor the appetite," Mama smiled discreetly as she turned back to the kitchen.

Emilia joined her inside, squinting in vague consternation at Mama's words. They worked side by side in the kitchen for a while when Mama stopped and turned to Emilia.

"What?" Emilia looked up.

Mama stood silently looking at her daughter as a soft smile grew on her face. "You are growing into a very strong and beautiful young woman." She stepped toward her, stroked her hair, slid her hands down to cup her daughter's cheeks, and finally rested them on her shoulders. "No matter what happens today, remember that your father and I both love you very much!"

"I know, Mama, but..." She put her hands on her mother's wrists and felt her face twist in frustration.

"I know, mija, but he *does* love you, more than you can know. And he's doing the very best he can for you, for us, for the community, *and* for the company. He has a responsibility to all of us. It's not easy for him."

"Mama, I know what they want to do! I've *seen* it!" The dam holding everything back inside Emilia's head had broken.

"What do you mean?"

"Well, a few days ago, I... Last night, Miguel and I saw that some trees were cut down near the park!"

"That's just part of the maintenance plan, Emilia. Why do you worry so much?"

"But the soup shed! There was damage. Somebody tried to break in!"

"Oh, no, it must be the animals. You know they're hungry and roaming this time of year. We'll bring up repairs today during the meeting. Don't worry, it will get fixed!"

"But..." Emilia started, then sighed, resigned to keep quiet or risk being misunderstood. She turned and wiped down the counters, remembering the agreement she made with Miguel to pick the right moment. This was not it. "Okay," she said. Knowing that it was *not* okay made the word sting as it left her mouth.

Mama spoke while smoothing, and brushing Emilia's straight, black hair from behind.

"There are many changes and challenges ahead for you, Emilia. But this is true for everyone. Keep that in mind as you and your friends decide how *your* lives will unfold."

"That's what Anzi says. Why doesn't *Papa* understand?"

Mama worked on fashioning two braids into Emilia's hair. "You know what I really think?" She lowered her voice to a mischievous whisper and leaned closer to Emilia's ear. "I think that perhaps the men have been in charge for a bit too long. They are sometimes blinded by their own nature and take on too much responsibility without any balance. I know about your afternoon away from work. I know it's something you needed to do and that you'll share when you're ready."

"You *know?* How?"

Into the end of each braid she twisted a fresh flower and then turned her daughter around. "Beautiful!" She kissed Emilia on the forehead and smiled with an unexpected comfort. "A mother knows. And while I haven't spoken with him yet, I have an idea about the things your grandfather may have shown you."

"You *do?* Mama, why didn't you tell me? Why doesn't everyone know? It's who we *are!*" Emilia's face twisted in consternation.

Mama sighed. "It's complicated; maybe you'll understand more sometime soon."

Emilia felt her insides clench up. She wanted to tell her mother just exactly how much she really knew if only to stop her from treating her like a child. The knock on the door brought an end to their moment and they both perked up with excitement.

Mama turned to the door to receive the guests, but paused briefly, turned back, and revealed a focus Emilia had not seen in her before. "Your adventuresome nature reminds me of myself when I was your age. I recognize your need to explore the world. But use your heart, Emilia, and your mind. I can see the balanced strength you carry in each. And so does your father. And Anzi, well, he is Anzi. I won't hold you back from your dreams, Emilia, now that you have met them." With that, she turned to meet her guests, leaving Emilia with an undefinable, inner disquiet.

Quickly wiping down the counters, Emilia ran upstairs to change. Putting on a simple white dress with colorful embroidery circling each hem, she recalled Anzi's words, *Knowing with feeling.* They were the same as her mother's words just now. Around her waist she wrapped a red cloth belt and wove her pouch full of teeth into a traditional tyet knot. The mirror she stood in front of reflected two images, only one of which she could see. The rich colors she wore on both her skin and her clothes were clear and crisp. Her physical features were shaped in part by genetics, in part by experience. But deeper within the soulful intensity reflected in her dark eyes, not yet fully revealed, was an overflowing palette of colors, shapes, and sounds formed by the intentions she carried within, released unseen into the living, kinetic art that she was.

12 – BELLA LUNA

The house filled with happy, chatty, brightly dressed people. They spilled in and out of the doors, gathering in and around the house. Many congregated in the back by the fire where all kinds of beverages and snacks were scattered throughout the din of talk and laughter. Papa and Miguel's father, Alonso, worked at uncovering and carving the roasted pig. Emilia ladled out another pot of soup from the kettle while chatting with friends from school and scanning the crowd for Miguel.

Everyone quieted and all eyes turned to Mama when she sprang into the crowd wielding a machete over her head and let out a loud, tuneful, "*WHOOOOP!*" She twirled around so her brightly decorated dress whirled up into a spinning color wheel. The crowd let out a cheer and moved into a circle with Mama at the center.

Arely relished the chance to show her skills and it made Emilia cringe a little, but smile a lot to watch this rare and refreshing departure from her role as, well, her mother. Seeing her like this, Emilia couldn't think of her as a parent, but rather as the person in the community named Arely who loved to dance flamboyantly. Her dance performance was legendary at Bella Luna. Mama said she learned it from her mother, who learned it from hers. Sometimes she did the dance with flaming batons. Emilia wondered how it was possible that she didn't inherit a single ounce of her mother's extroverted performer genes.

Arely stopped and briefly curtsied, then raised both arms straight up into the air, chin high, and turned slowly around, hips and knees bouncing in rhythm as if counting into a song. The crowd cheered in anticipation. Someone pushed "play" on the tape machine and the music started. People clapped in time to the beat and Arely dropped one arm to point at the crowd as she circled around. The machete in her other hand was still pointed high in the sky, directly at the sun. Finally, she dropped the machete from overhead and caught it in her lower hand to start the dance. Spinning around fast enough for the rainbow dress to balloon like an umbrella, her long hair whipped along behind. She raised the machete over her head and twirled it around rapidly in her hand like a baton. The crowd backed up to a safe distance, letting out collective *"Ooohhs"* and, *"Aahhhs!"*.

Arely moved fast, weaving the machete through her fingers, then around her back. All through the dance she moved slowly toward the giant loaf of push bread with the crowd still clapping and cheering, morphing around her movements. She tossed the machete straight up, spinning high into the air while her feet continued to stomp out the ancient dance in rhythmic, spiraling circles, dress spinning in a blur, feet sliding, stomping, and skipping, never letting her piercing eyes unlock from the potentially deadly knife. Music and shouts filled the air. She stepped sideways, arm outstretched, keeping perfect time with the beat, one more half-spin aligned her perfectly to grab the falling machete by the handle and in one smooth motion spun it around and down, slamming it through the bread, cleanly lopping off a large chunk and bringing a cheer from the onlookers. The machete remained lodged in the wooden peel under the bread while Arely danced flamboyantly for another minute to the cheering, clapping crowd. She stopped, smiling from ear to ear, arms out, ankles crossed, and out of breath. The crowd roared with delight! She pulled the machete out of the peel with one hand, picked up the hunk of bread with the other, and raised them both up over her head. She turned a full circle smiling, curtsying, and soaking up cheers, hoots, and applause as she did.

"Bella Luna!" she called, hunk of bread in one hand, machete in the other. *"Let's eat!"*

The crowd cheered once again and Mama retreated inside with both bread and machete. Emilia soon followed with a pot of soup but took her time, in part because the pot was so heavy, but mostly because she was looking around and through the crowd for Miguel. Anzi held the door.

"Thanks, Anzi."

"Of course!" he replied and helped her lift the pot to the countertop.

Inside, where most of the grandparents were gathering, the atmosphere was a bit more subdued than outside. For the moment, they were alone in the kitchen but it wouldn't last. Guests soon saw the soup and bread and started moving toward it.

"I have a funny feeling about today, Anzi," Emilia said quietly, stirring the soup and feeling an odd mix of concern and bemusement.

"Whatever happens, you will not be alone," he squeezed her shoulder and smiled. She felt a warm tingle from Anzi's hand that radiated down her arm and into her chest. He added, "Do not worry, he will be here!" he winked, she winced, they laughed. "I have something for you." From inside his vest, Anzi took the necklace and put it around her neck. "A gift from both of us."

She held it up and massaged the four large bear teeth hanging from the cord. Her eyes beamed and her heart swelled. She threw her arms around her grandfather, kissing his leathery, milk-shaven cheek. The line for the soup was forming. The necklace made her feel different somehow. Special, more confident. She checked her eyes with the palms of her hands and looked at Anzi once more. They threw sparks at each other that only they could see, making them both laugh. She then reached for the ladle and began the cheerful duty of serving the first several guests in line, smiling, chatting, and feeling especially solid within herself. The hot soup was sipped and slurped, followed by exclamations of how excellent it was this year and detailed comparisons with previous years.

Outside, the party roared with music, singing, shouts, and laughter. Some wore colorful animal masks, some had painted faces, and there was plenty of shiny jewelry. Random hoots and hollers peppered the general ruckus. Inside, the house was crowded with the older generations sipping soup, telling stories, and sharing memories. Emilia straddled the doorway, crossing back and forth, feeling equally drawn to the happenings and energy on each side of the wall, craning her neck each and every way for a glimpse of Miguel. She was also surprised that Toro and his friends didn't show up. With their parents here, they would be on their best behavior, as low a bar as that might be. She began to wonder and worry if there was some unhappy connection between these absences.

"We traded our land *and* our values for a little money and a *lot* of Bigly's empty promises!" She heard the accusation fly from inside, walked closer and stood quietly at the edge of the simmering pot of conversational stew where steam was starting to rise. She felt a little guilty for being happy about this and kept her smile on the inside.

"He is working for *all* of us! *I* am working for all of *you*, you know that!" Papa's voice was firm, authoritative. The inside crowd quieted to listen.

"Yes, Ernesto, you are! And I, for one, am grateful. You've negotiated well with Tode. We all can see that, can't we? Is there anyone else who would like that job?" Alonso and Ernesto grew up together and were inseparable friends. There was light laughter and a shaking of heads; Papa relaxed in the support.

"He enslaved us, *and* our culture!" The woman's voice was old but strong, "You youngsters don't remember how things were. Our lives and memories are just stories to you, like make-believe!" She looked at Ernesto and back to her son.

"Mother, *please*," Alonso tried to speak, but Gabriela did not offer him the space.

"We did not know then what we had to lose when those papers were signed!" she continued. "Isn't that right, Manuel?" She looked sternly at Anzi who nodded slowly in agreement followed by a murmur of acknowledgement among the elders. "You and my Philipé, rest his soul, and the rest of the Council of that day, did not listen to your wise women! Now there are fewer birds in our trees and our health suffers from the poisons we must apply to those coffee plants!"

"Yes! The soil is *ruined*!" came a shout. "Anything I plant withers and dies!"

"It's true!" More murmurs and light applause sprinkled among the crowd.

"And what of our time? The park is empty now," Gabriela added. "Everyone's working all the time."

This was not turning out to be the usual reminiscing Emilia was hoping for and she began to feel a little anxious.

"Now... friends..." Papa held up his hand to quiet the commotion, "I intended to address these issues at our business meeting. Can we put this aside for the moment?"

"Why wait? Start the meeting now!" Gabriela's insistence was supported by almost all of the old-timers.

Ernesto looked at Alonzo but all he could do was shrug his shoulders.

"We cannot start the meeting without a formal call to action," said Ernesto. "But you've put me on the spot, and I'll do my best to informally help us move through this awkward phase of our plan."

"Well, at least there's a plan!" a man said to his friend, but loud enough for all to hear.

"Friends," Ernesto began, "you miss the old ways, I know, I understand! And we're grateful for all you've done to keep our venerable history alive. Together, we have kept our community strong. But we have to think of our future, our *children's* future!"

Papa was sincere and very diplomatic, as usual, but it seemed that his plan for an organized presentation had given over to the winds of fomenting passion. Unless he could get things quickly back on track, there would be no meeting and the speech he had spent so much time preparing would be useless. This made him impatient and, as Emilia knew well, impatience would stand in opposition to his planned eloquence and well-considered words. She felt nervous for her father, and yet eager for the conversation about to come.

"There is work here in our village now," he continued, holding a level tone, "*Real* work that will provide for us *and* our families far into the future! Our children should not need to move to the city to find jobs!" Applause followed this remark. "The opportunities we are creating today will move us steadily and assuredly into the modern world!"

"What has the modern world given us except the destruction of our land?" a voice called out.

"And our culture!" sounded another

"It has brought us money!" A young man leaned in through the window from outside waving his cell phone and smiling.

People were starting to trickle inside, drawn by the commotion.

"We're connected to the world now!" another young voice announced.

Many shouts of appreciation and applause followed this comment, mostly from the younger crowd outside.

"The money you earn comes at a far greater cost to all of us! And all you want is more and more of it! There's already too much damage! It's not worth it!" Gabriela's voice filled with passion.

"What would you do now?" Frustration rose in Ernesto's voice and Emilia's chest tightened. "What would you have *me* do now? We can't just turn back around, we're too far down this path and *we are committed to it!* Even if we were to go back to the old ways *this very minute*, it would take *years* to bear fruit, decades! We would perish. We have all worked too hard, *I* have worked too hard. We are working for something *together.*" He raised a fist. "Something that will lift us all to a higher standard of living!"

"Yes! We need this!" Alonso called out in support.

"Whose standards? Yours, not mine!" dissent mounted and divided the room.

Without planning to say anything, the words simply escaped from her. The moment had suddenly, startlingly arrived for Emilia to add her own truth. "I would rather have my garden and our culture than all the money I could ever earn from working in coffee fields!" The room went silent. Not even Emilia could believe the resolve of the words that came in a steady, sturdy stream from her own mouth. And there were more just behind those that couldn't be stopped. "I don't want to give over my life to work for goals that aren't mine, for values I don't believe in." She glanced at Papa, who wore a perplexed look mixed with his last hold on calm authority. She instantly wanted to apologize, but could not do so with sincerity. She was glad she said what she did; it was the truth, and there was no turning back. Her eyes darted around the silent room looking for support and quickly landed on Anzi. She recalled past words of his: *"Safety does not take us to places we need to explore."*

Her heart pounded, the bear teeth rose and fell on her chest, eyes transfixed in Anzi's intense gaze as if the two of them stood alone in the room. What happened next she could never have anticipated. Every single memory, every detail of the past week flooded into her all at once. She saw and felt it all. Looking into the skeleton's eyes, then out at the clear, deep ocean from within the giant Bear's eyes, no telling how far down the bottom was, she could go anywhere, as deep as she wanted, breathing water like it was air. She felt the waves at the thundering ear crash over her again and again. Suddenly, a flash of blinding light, a swirling tunnel of fog, lightning, and stars opened in front of her, making her tingle from head to toe with static electricity. And just as in last night's dream, just as real and solid as her own self, Calista appeared out of the tempest and walked right into her, lingering so that they each shared the same space. She was buzzing with the sting of a thousand scorpions. The room sped across eternity, twisting end over end through the stormy tunnel. Then, just as quickly, the tunnel snapped closed and jolted her back to now. Emilia took a half step backward to regain the balance the vision had sapped from her. She felt herself stamp each foot on the ground.

Everyone was still looking just as if no time at all had passed. She was the only one who had seen anything, the only one who knew. Anzi winked and smiled; of course, he knew. But this time Emilia didn't wince at his magical sparkle or look away. Instead, she looked squarely into that light, smiled, and winked back at him. Again she felt herself growing from the inside, and again her legs became more solid beneath her. The scorpion sting buzz subsided but did not disappear. Rather than the painful sting she felt the first time, it now radiated a warm vibration throughout her.

A loud squeal from outside grabbed everyone's attention away from the silence. Miguel's bicycle brakes announced his arrival, followed by a crash as he jumped off the bike and it hit the ground. Emilia ran to the open door as Miguel ran inside, sweating and out of breath. All eyes were on him now, for which Emilia was grateful. But her relief was held at bay by his troubled look.

"*They're here!* I mean, they're *there!*" he panted, waving his arms frantically, "At the park! *Hurry!*"

"Miguel, what *are* you talking about?" his father asked.

"Are you okay?!" Emilia reached for his hand. "Calm down, tell us what you saw!"

He took a deep breath. "Okay. I was riding around town, on my way here. I rode by the park and I saw them!"

"*Who* did you see?" Alonso was anxious about his son's odd behavior.

"*Caláco*! Their men! The machines! They're going crazy! I hid and watched them, but then I couldn't leave without being noticed, so I just stayed. They were talking and looking at plans or something, big papers." He stretched out his arms and inadvertently knocked over a basket of fruit that Emilia was able to quickly catch and put back. "They walked around the entire place, pointing and planning and looking at the papers. Then they got chainsaws and started cutting down trees! That's what *you* saw, right Em?" He looked at her with imploring eyes. "That's when I ran. The machines are wrecking the place! I think they're gonna tear down the bandstand! We have to *do* something!"

"Ernesto! You are the senior supervisor, what do you know of this?" a voice accused.

"Nothing! Surely they are only doing some required maintenance work. That is part of our arrangement. I will speak with the director on Monday morning. Now, if we can..."

"This *isn't* maintenance! *Monday will be too late!* We have to do something *now*!" Miguel was adamant and couldn't believe that everyone didn't rush out to stop them.

"Miguel, are you sure?" his father asked in his most authoritative way.

"Of *course* I am! I wouldn't make this up! Why would I?" his voice cracked under the strain. He hated that he always had to work to get people to believe him.

"Sometimes parents forget that their children are no longer five years old with overactive imaginations," Mama spoke up looking sympathetically at Miguel, then back to her husband.

"Yes, why would you?" Alonso acquiesced. "Ernesto?" He turned to his friend, "What do you propose?"

"If this is true, there must be some misunderstanding," said Ernesto.

Miguel rolled his eyes and huffed, "It's *true*! We need to *do* something and *fast*!"

"Very well. Alonso, you and I will go investigate," said Ernesto. "We'll report back soon. I'm sure there's a simple explanation. The rest of you, please, you are my guests, please stay and enjoy yourselves! We'll start the meeting when we return and continue with our feast!"

The Biggest Bear

Ernesto and Alonso struggled through the crowd toward the door but didn't make it. The room was now filled beyond its walls, the window frames filled with faces looking in from outside. Whispers and murmurs escalated into loud voices, accusations, and confusion. Miguel squeezed Emilia's hand looking urgently at her. She looked back, eyes wide, and silently mouthed, "*I know!*"

Anzi stood at the front of the room, banged his Staff of Ceremony loudly twice on the floor, then raised it into the air. The Staff might have been as old as the soup. Its top was carved as a bear head, the worn shank held embedded bear claws, eagle talons, various gemstones, and it was adorned with fur and feathers. Its presence invoked the reverence of antiquity and authority. Its effect was immediate; nobody could ignore the Staff, or Anzi, and the two of them together were a call for the highest respect. The room went silent. Papa looked longingly at the Staff. It should have been in his hands by now, giving him the authority to present his report and the case for progress.

"We did not know then what we had to lose when those papers were signed. What Gabriela said is true," Anzi began. "My beloved Maria also knew this truth, and now the noise and destruction from the earth-eating, smoke-belching monsters draws near. This is not what our ancestors wanted; this is not the legacy they left for us, nor is it what I wish to leave for my granddaughter, or for yours." He turned to his son, closed his eyes, and tipped his head in a gesture of respect. "I do apologize for this unfoldment, Ernesto. With all due respect, will you allow me to continue?"

Ernesto nodded back and gestured with his hand to offer continuation. It was his only choice.

"I am not proud, but I am no longer ashamed," Anzi continued, now addressing the crowd. "We thought we were doing what was best for our families when we made agreements between the village and Caláco. What has transpired these past years is far outside the boundaries of our understanding of that original agreement. Slowly they have tightened the noose that we tied with them. We must be careful with our accusations, though. We are no different than they. We grew complacent in our greed while they took advantage of us in theirs. We traded our land, our values, for empty promises. We stood by, hardly noticing that we had been captured and enslaved along with our traditions, allowing both to be changed."

With a nod and an outstretched arm, he motioned for Emilia to join him, handed her the Staff, and just as quietly he was seated. The crowd collectively inhaled in a subdued gasp, looking at each other silently with confusion on their faces, wondering if the old man had finally gone senile.

Emilia stood alone, her hand shaking as she reached for the Staff, not knowing exactly what Anzi expected of her, or she of herself. By being called to speak she was riding on the back of her grandfather's reputation. And, she had to account for herself in front of her father. In front of everyone. She couldn't screw this up. Once the Staff was in her hand she steadied immediately, growing tall inside. Again she learned that saying *yes* invited the unknown, and again her next move revealed itself clearly only after accepting the *yes* of the moment. She understood the urgency of now more than anyone, and had to trust that each step would unfold like a dance she was just now learning. She also knew her audience enough to recognize that some would need to be convinced before taking action, and having everyone on board would be essential. She took a deep breath, closed her eyes, and drew on the insights she had been given this week. With a brief, apologetic and reverent nod to her father, she began.

"Friends, those of you who know me know that my curiosity often gets the better of my intentions." A few chuckles from the audience lightened the mood a bit. "A few days ago I went off to follow a noise. You've all heard it, that rumbly, growling noise off in the distance. I remember the stories my parents told, and some of you told, too," she looked around the room, eyes stopping on those to whom she referred, "when I was younger, about a monster, a big bear that was out there somewhere. I think it was only told to scare children into being good or the bear would come and get you!" Emilia mimicked an angry bear face and held her free hand like a claw. More chuckles and nods of agreement were shared among parents and grandparents. "Well, friends, I have seen the so-called bear monster and learned both the truth *and* the lie behind it!" Her voice was strong, steady and determined.

The crowd whispered but soon went silent and focused again on Emilia. Many of the younger people tilted their heads with the mystery of it and listened hard. She left many details out, but related her sadness and anger over losing her garden, expressed her irresistible compulsion to find the source of the faint noise she heard so many times, the far off singing and how it made her feel that she belonged to a community of family and friends who knew and loved her, even if they didn't always agree. Her voice steadied and rose, hands gesturing as she recounted the tale, and brief tears came as she spoke of the tearing of the earth by the smoking monster. She quickly wiped away the tears and replaced them with fierceness. She grew again. Her audience was rapt as she offered tiny tidbits of her adventure with Anzi.

"Anzi told me everything," she said, addressing the old timers. "I understand that you thought you were doing the best thing for us. But it didn't work. They're taking advantage of us; they've been doing it for years and they're doing it even now as we speak! If we let them continue, we will disappear into them, there will be no more community, no more us. But yes, there will be plenty of work. The problem is, we will only be working for *them*, never for ourselves."

While she spoke, Emilia became more animated. An artful beauty flowed from inside of her, like lava from inside the earth creating new land, radiating the strength and hope of a young woman who could no longer suppress her intense passion for life. Her final words to the group were calm and resolute, "Miguel is telling the truth. We've both seen it. And trust me, there is more about us than most of you know! There are many ancient secrets hidden in plain sight within our village that have been ignored, stolen, or forgotten. We're here today not just for a party, but to honor the Bear, our ancient Calista, and our ancestors who brought us to this moment." She paused and scanned the crowd, holding the attention of each and every person. She inhaled deeply, "Friends, it's time for us to *take back the bear!*" She handed the Staff back to her grandfather. He stood to receive it. The Staff was always returned to the one who presented it.

"The truth," he confirmed, "from our young warrior."

The room went silent. Then the elders, most of them sitting together, started whispering among themselves. Regardless of what they thought about progress, what it was or wasn't, they had all seen the ways of their ancient village and its people slowly disappear in their lifetimes. Now, standing in front of them was the greatest force of both destruction and revelation. Truth. Absolute, inarguable, truth. They could no longer hide from the truth of how they were manipulated over the years, or their shame for being complicit in their own demise. Each one knew that the call had finally come to end the lies.

Gabriela could not contain her fire any longer and stood up. "Many of you youngsters may still believe that the bear is a monster," she pointed out a few of the children in the crowd. "I blame myself, *and all the rest of you old cowards!*" She raised her voice, banged her cane on the floor and waved her free arm around the room. "There were days – and not too long ago," she pointed her bony finger up over her head and continued, "when we could hear the secrets of the earth and of the winds. They flowed through us like water and lit us up like *fire!* And this Feast for our Bella Luna was how we honored the generosity of nature, of life itself. Now Emilia, our wise and fearless young warrior for truth has reminded us! And Miguel, where are you, Miguel?" She bounced on her tiptoes, trying to get a view over taller heads and finally acknowledged him directly. "Our young Miguel has seen the immediate threat that has resulted from the long lies and came to warn us. We must be united! Emilia is correct. Calista is no monster! She is strong, proud, fearless, and resolute. Whether you think she is myth or real, *she is us!*" She banged her cane loudly on the metal chair and put her fist against her heart. "And she is *here!*" She turned to Emilia saying firmly, "She is *you*." The crowd responded with hoots, yips, and applause. "We have ignored ourselves for *too - long*. The time to act is *now!* I am with Emilia, *Take back the bear!*" Gabriela moved to stand next to Emilia, who was holding Miguel's hand, and standing next to Anzi. "Who will stand with us?!"

People began to whisper, and the whisper quickly became a roar, and the roar became a song when the entire crowd stood cheering and chanting, "TAKE BACK THE BEAR! *TAKE BACK THE BEAR!*"

Anzi rested his hand on Emilia's shoulder and raised his Staff high, steadfast and confident looking out to the chanting crowd. Emilia turned to Papa who looked as though he was facing a tsunami. She reached out her hand to him. His choice now was to become a part of the wave, or drown in it. She felt herself growing yet again, centered squarely over feet that solidly anchored her body to the ground while her heart was tethered to the light of the sun. No wind could sway her. Something that felt like destiny was opening a locked door to which she had turned an inadvertent key. She held her eyes on Papa, who reached out and took her hand.

They spilled out of the house and yard, funneling into the street as a single living organism. Some ran, some walked, but they were all of a single mind.

13 – THE BIGGEST BEAR

Emilia walked quickly within the flowing, shape-shifting crowd along with her parents and Anzi. Some were still chanting, and the few who had cell phones made calls to spread the word. If they didn't think Bella Luna was important enough to attend, then at least maybe this was. Miguel jogged up next to her.

"*There* you are!" said Emilia.

"You are *un*-believable!" said Miguel, eyes wide. "Take back the *bear*!? Where did that even come from?"

"I couldn't believe it my*self*, Miguel! I hardly even *feel* like myself, but it's strange, I've never felt *more* like myself!"

"There's more," Miguel said.

"What?! Tell me!"

"Toro was there, and the others, at the park. Do you think they really went to the mountain? To check them out? I mean, when you said that to them yesterday?"

"I don't know. I really wanted them to go see for themselves, but I wasn't sure if they really had the guts to do anything other than be bullies. What did you see?"

"I couldn't tell really, exactly. They were kind of in the woods." Miguel lowered his voice a little, "It almost seemed like they were kind of... maybe, like working with them?"

"*What?!* Those... *Aahhhgg!*" Emilia stomped the ground hard. "Tell me exactly what you saw them doing."

"Well, it seemed like they were working on the machines, maybe filling up the gas tanks or fixing them or something."

"Those... those *traitors!*" Emilia fumed, then calmed. "Okay, we'll just do what we need to do to stop them."

"How?"

Emilia thought quickly. "Miguel, have you ever danced in the dark?"

"Yeah, right, I can't even dance in the daylight! What do you mean?"

"Well, I can't explain it really, but you know how you say you just always seem to be in the right place and everything works itself out?"

"Yeah... but..." This whole concept was not yet clearly formed in Miguel's mind. He had no idea how it worked or if it was just coincidence, so he certainly didn't trust it to be real.

"It's kind of like that; just follow my lead and don't think too hard. Put one foot down at a time. A place will open up, and you'll know." Emilia's confidence was comforting, even if his own was not.

"Sounds kind of vague, but okay. What do you think they're gonna do?"

"I don't know, but they *can't* take down the bandstand! I hope we're not too late!"

They reached the edge of the park where the crowd was already bigger than the one from the party. People at the front jumped and shouted amid the noise of machines. All they could see as they approached was the black soot of rising exhaust.

"What's happening? I can't see!" Emilia bounced on her tiptoes, craning her neck from side to side.

Miguel jumped up a few times to get a better view over the crowd "It looks like, wait, I don't see it," he shouted. "I don't see the bandstand!"

The urgency of those words filled Emilia to bursting. Her body was suddenly at full throttle and her brain in overdrive. She broke loose and pushed her legs into a sprint, darting around and through the crowd. She was moving more than thinking, propelled again by stubborn and self-serving feet that took the rest of her body along for the ride without asking permission. By the time Miguel turned to look, she was gone. He tried to follow, but quickly lost sight of her.

With a great roar and belching of smoke, a giant yellow arm swung out into the crowd, causing them to shout in unison and quickly reverse direction like a murmuration of birds turning in flight. Emilia moved with the determination of an avalanche, finding holes in the crowd and darting through them.

She stared in horrified disbelief at the bandstand now lying in rubble. Rage formed an anguished scream, obliterating any room for fear. The machine clattered slowly along its trail of devastation. Several more of the same large machines sat idling and men with chainsaws stopped cutting to watch the growing crowd. She scanned the entire scene with one eye and kept the other on the moving machine. All the brush and trees that once obscured the soup shed were now lying on the ground, offering a clear view of the shed and beyond. A few people were visible in the distance through the smoke, dust, and remaining trees. It seemed like a scuffle was breaking out among them. Squinting, she could see that one of them was Toro, and it looked like he was swinging a stick at someone. *What are they up to? Fighting among themselves now? Way to go, boys,* she thought. More figures quickly arrived next to Toro.

A map started to form in her head, like she was looking down from up high and the entire scene became clear in her mind's eye. Men and machines were scattered about beyond the crowd. Toro, his stick, and his friends were on one side, and the man he was waving the stick at reached to his side and pointed his arm toward them. The boys scattered, the man fired a shot into the air. The crowd let out a collective gasp. The machines stopped moving. Gun-wielding men quickly appeared and stood against the now angry mob. Another collective scream, a few people crouched down low, but nobody ran. Then everyone quieted and moved tentatively, in shock at what they were witnessing, unsure of what to expect or do. They realized they were powerless against the dire circumstance of machines, weapons, and unknown motivations.

Emilia watched as Papa moved to the front of the crowd and shouted for Tode, Alonso by his side. Nobody was looking in her direction and she took the opportunity to sprint for cover behind one of the few remaining trees and piles of brush scattered on the ground. She had to get closer to the soup shed, one dance step at a time. There was no way she would let them knock that down next!

"Tode!" Ernesto shouted, "What's going on here! What is this? What are you doing to our park?"

"Maintenance!" shouted Tode through the din of the idling machines.

"What maintenance? You told me nothing of *this*!" he gestured with outstretched arms.

"I don't need to tell you *anything*. Get back or get hurt! *All* of you!"

"This was not in any agreement we had with Caláco. Explain this action!" Anzi demanded from his son's side.

Tode laid his plan well and was prepared for this contingency. He would use their own words against them, even if they were decades old words. He reached for a copy of the contract stuffed inside his jacket, already folded to the page where the section in need was highlighted.

"See here," said Tode, waving the page in front of them. He read aloud, "Page seventeen, paragraph five, section A, whereas all additional work deemed necessary for the satisfactory completion of all projects heretofore mentioned or otherwise disregarded or not specifically specified until such time as deemed relevant by the developing agent or agents shall be undertaken in the most expeditious and timely manner at the sole discretion of said developing agent." He looked up from the document. "That means we get to do what we want, when we want."

"That is not what we signed, and it is certainly *not* in the spirit of our agreement!" Anzi was incredulous.

"Save your sermon for church, old man, there's more." Tode raised the paper again, shaking it in Anzi's face as he did. "Having received sufficient remuneration for this, and or other, clause, or clauses, specified or unspecified, the signatories do hereby relinquish ownership of aforementioned properties. Signed," he turned the paper to face Anzi, "is this not your mark? And the marks of your representatives?"

"It is my mark. But that was not our understanding of the agreement! You are a thief!" Anzi stood fast against the adversary.

"Out of the way, old man! This is a *work* zone!" Tode unexpectedly lashed out an arm and shoved Anzi who tumbled onto his backside.

The crowd jeered but made no moves against the armed men.

Ernesto clenched his fists with rage and shouted, "TOOODE! YOU..." He pulled back his right arm to strike a blow when the men on either side of Tode trained their guns on him. One side of Tode's face lifted in a condescending smirk.

Ernesto withdrew his loaded fist and turned to help steady his father. Weapons were now trained on each of them.

"Go back to your fantasy party!" Tode sneered, "And be on time for work tomorrow!" He waved his pistol in the air and turned back to his destruction. He motioned for the driver to continue, and the clattering and smoke began again, this time heading directly toward the soup shed.

Emilia saw everything but remained unnoticed, staying low and moving steadily, dashing and darting for cover behind fallen tree limbs. Her fury at seeing her grandfather knocked down only strengthened her resolve to do the same to this whole operation. There was no other option except action. Her feet were moving once again, her mind anchored securely to perfect, momentary insight.

She burst into a sprint and raced out from behind cover, quickly catching up and passing the giant, belching, yellow terror. She moved boldly, propelled by the solid force of all her will. The world seemed to be moving in slow motion all around her as she gained on the dawdling mechanical giant. She could feel the bear claws against her skin, could hear the roar of the thundering ear, she felt everything around her as though everything was part of her and took a deep breath as if about to dive deeply underwater. With all the noise and fury of the roaring surf, unable to stop herself as a wave is unable to halt its steady advance and inexorable crash upon the beach, Emilia raced at top speed and took a flying leap. She flowed through the air as if in a dream where she could fly and finally landed directly in front of the soup shed. Time was not available in which to pause and question. Her comparatively tiny form now stood in the path of approaching destruction. She remained still and firm, feet anchored wide, arms stretched out and above, so she stood like a star. Breathing deeply, blazing eyes open wide, her entire being radiated defiance. The machine came to a stop. Everyone turned to watch this spectacle of absurdity.

"*Emilia!*" her mother screamed at the top of her lungs. "RUN!"

"You'll be *killed*, child!" Papa shouted. He ran toward her until a warning shot rang out and the guns were again trained on him. "Emilia, *run!*" he shouted. Shouting was all he could do. He felt sick inside.

There were many calls and cries but all of them sounded to Emilia as though they were unintelligible whispers from the other side of a dream. She could not move. Her feet had grown roots and her ground was claimed. There was no fear, and the feeling of fullness in her belly returned, radiating out to fill every cell in her body. She was, in that moment, every thread that made up the living tapestry of all the bones in the ossuary. She was every song ever sung; every ingredient ever stirred into the soup. She heard Gabriela's voice in her head, *She is you.* Emilia inhaled those words by thought alone and they filled her up. She imagined the bony white Calista standing watch atop the cliff. She stretched and stood as tall as she could, letting out a piercing, "STO-O-O-OP!!!"

The machine stopped. Tode and his men stared in disbelief, looked at each other, then burst into laughter. The machine lurched forward and the crowd reacted with angry shouts and terrified screams. Crawling closer to Emilia and the shed, it lifted its giant iron arm up high. She opened her mouth to yell again. It was all she could do. But no piercing shout was available to her. Her body buzzed with the scorpion electricity of clutching Calista's paw, but more. She held that power close, not shaking loose of it, allowing it to feed her growing fullness. Right now, the thought of backing down was the only thing that scared her. Her vision expanded again offering the perspective of looking down from overhead, and this time it seemed like she was watching a play; a play that she was directing, but where there was no script, and the characters had their own free will to improvise. But she knew the story somehow, she could feel it.

The mighty force of wind carried in her belly built up and unleashed a resounding roar that echoed and quieted everyone except the machine. "STO-O-O-OP!!!" She stomped the earth firmly, replanting each foot, again claiming this ground as hers.

Her next words came without a thought, without a script. They were clear and deliberate. And they were loud, "I AM THE BIGGEST BEAR!!" She grew ten feet tall as she spoke. "YOU ARE *NOTHING* AND YOU STOP *HERE!!*" The hurricane voice was fierce, resonating clearly over the clattering din of the machine.

As the words left her mouth, a tremendous thing happened. Emilia realized that when you see a thing for what it really is, and call it so, its power shrinks and becomes yours. Truth is owned only by truth.

The crowd watched in speechless disbelief, their mouths open, united in their collectively frozen breath, stunned by this audacious sight. Everyone, that is, except Anzi, whose whole being was beaming at his beautiful granddaughter. He tried hard not to smile in his delight for her, for doing so would invite misunderstanding from others. It was a grave situation, and he knew that only she could define this moment, a moment that was already building the future.

The machine driver, not truly wanting to hurt the girl in front of him, was confounded in his mission by what he saw and heard. Both of them stood still breathing smoke and fire at each other. The machine's engine roared with intimidation, and then sputtered. The driver looked at Tode, who knew it would be best if nobody got hurt, but he could not afford to show weakness. He briefly weighed the option of putting a driver into another machine to ensure success but decided that the men were more effective where they were: holding back the angry crowd. Tode waved his gun indicating to the driver that he should keep moving. *The girl will move,* he was sure.

The machine roared and spat hot black clouds of smoke and fire, clanking back into motion. It sputtered again and slowed briefly. Its mighty metal claw lashed out at her but stopped short of where she stood when the driver saw she wasn't going to move.

"*YOUR STEAM DOES NOT SCALD!*" She hurled emboldened words upon the mighty gale of her voice, unable to speak in anything but a deafening roar now. The powerful but slow-moving monster lurched forward. Emilia danced her way around it while it spun, reached, and grabbed at her. She would not let it advance any further.

Once again, she grew and boomed, "*I AM THE BIGGEST BEAR!*" It felt good deep down inside of her to say this and feel it resonate so thoroughly within and throughout her. She said it again, pausing for a moment to make the point by standing tall, raising her arms high overhead, looking to the sky and stomping the ground with all her newfound strength and determined intention. *"I - AM - THE - BIGGEST - BEAR!!"* Girl and bear each embodied the other. A trick of light animated the teeth on her necklace, making them appear to dance and jump as they rose and fell steadily on her chest.

And then a second beautiful thing happened. Emilia found that when one calls upon her power and fully claims it, it becomes her own. She reveled in the satisfaction of this new truth.

Emilia vaguely heard the shouts of people who had moved in more closely now, frantically trying to distract the driver's attention away from her. The machine turned and swiped its giant arm at the crowd to hold them back. They feared for their lives, but more for Emilia and so could not just turn and run. Yet despite the fear and disbelief in what they were witnessing, they hoped for her continued strength and agility, so they held their ground along with their breath as they watched in continued astonishment.

She stood strong, eyes closed, arms crossed over her chest now, breathing deeply as if to recharge. The driver took advantage of Emilia's self-absorbed distraction to advance unencumbered. He was finally close enough to take aim. The machine slowed, sputtered, and choked several times but managed to haul back its long arm, ready for the strike. A single blow would obliterate the shed. Then the engine choked and stalled. The driver cranked the starter, pumped the throttle hard, and the engine sputtered to life again.

Emilia could see everything in her mind's eye with a perspective from high above. She gulped huge lungfuls of air as if it was pure, energetic sustenance. Still inside of the same dream with everything moving in slow motion, she reached to her waist, into the tyet where hard teeth hung from her past in the small leather bag. She massaged them looking for something soft, like hope. She needed this last, potentially dangerous moment of indulgence to fully acknowledge her new power, to completely and incontrovertibly own it. *"I AM THE BIGGEST BEAR!"* Her steady, reverberating roar of words grew this time in every way, most importantly in its determination.

13 – The Biggest Bear

She said it again, even louder, *"I AM THE BIGGEST BEAR,"* and began to move with renewed focus. Her own words brought her out of distraction and opened her eyes to the moment that so desperately needed her. She could no longer allow men and machines to harm her friends, her family, her entire way of life and their shared history. There was no way she could live with herself if anyone got hurt, no way she could stand the loss of the ancient soup, and no *way* she was going to let anyone mess with her grandfather, *ever* again! Her own life seemed an insignificant matter compared to these. There was no more time to be enamored by her newfound confidence.

A sudden, blinding flash caught her eye and guided her through an instant that sharpened her mind and strengthened her resolve. She knew exactly what to do, exactly what she was capable of. She ran toward the flash. Anzi had maneuvered his way through all the commotion and was now standing still, holding the Staff of Ceremony up high. Their eyes locked as she ran. Sparks flew between them as she snatched the electrified Staff out of his hand. She was moving at a speed that seemed blindingly fast to the crowd, but painfully slow to her. Anzi and the Staff sealed both her confidence and her power and she *leapt* at the huge, sputtering, smoking monster!

And now a third incredible thing happened. As Emilia launched herself in full commitment to face the angry iron beast, she felt herself growing ever bigger and her power seemed boundless. The moment her feet left the ground, her head grew ten times in size and her body stretched out until it became longer even than the giant machine below. Her hands and feet grew huge with claws, her nose became a wet snout and she was fur all over. She had become her own dream.

"I AM CALISTA AND I STILL LIVE!" she boomed in a deafening thunder as she flew high above the moving monster. She circled and sighted in on the swinging claw now rising up to swipe her down. As she flew and grew, the belt around her waist snapped. She watched helplessly as the leather pouch plummeted to the ground and all the teeth Anzi patiently collected and saved over many years scattered down to the scarred earth. Her sadness at

losing something so precious seemed to propel her even more forcefully. There were no more touchstones to the life she knew, not even her own body. There was only this moment to be in; to be all in, as deep as the need.

Legs outstretched, claws extended, she lunged straight down with a mighty force and struck the beast. The Staff was jolted from her paw by the blow and she clung to the long, heavy, extended arm, tipping the whole machine over onto one tread, then rocking it back onto the other. She swung around the beast, hanging on for all she was worth as they rocked, swayed, and tipped in opposition to each other.

There was no outcome for her other than to ensure its defeat at all cost and so she did not let go. Her immense body spun, thrashed, and dragged the massive machine around in a relentless, timeless duel. The machine sputtered again, gasping into silence and finally tipped beyond its balance point. As it tipped over, she lost her grip, tumbling end over end, landing in a cloud of dust with a boom and a thud followed by clattering, smashing, clanking, smoke, and screaming. The machine toppled over, crashing down on top of her. Everything went black.

The crowd roared, jeered, cheered, and screamed as they swarmed the entangled creatures. The huge metal arm of the machine lay on top of the motionless Emilia. People tried lifting it off of her but could not. They grabbed logs and attempted to lever it up to free her, but it was too heavy. They didn't know how she could survive with the machine still on top of her.

Her head tilted to the side. Her eyes twitched and blinked open. The shimmer of the sinking sun was carried on a ripple of water in Anzi's sparkling eyes. They exchanged tired smiles that held the substance of their shared experience. His hand was on her head. There were no words available, and none were required. She turned her head; her parents each held one of her hands.

There was a stillness within Emilia despite the commotion all around her as people frantically tried to lift the machine off of her. Tode himself ran for an excavator, knowing it was the only thing that could lift the machine's bucket arm enough to get her out from under it.

"I love you so much, Emilia!" said Mama, throwing her arms around her neck, then stroking her cheeks and hair. "You'll be fine; help is on the way!" She kissed her cheek.

Papa held back tears, smiling with soft undying love. "I am so very proud of you, my daughter." He squeezed her hand tightly. "You know that I love you more than anything in the world. Today you are no longer mine," he smiled with shining eyes. "You have become a child of the village. We are all indebted to you for your courage and strength and for what you have taught us, what you have taught me."

Emilia cast a beam of light into Papa's eyes, then Mama's. She clutched the claw necklace, now tight around her neck, and remembered her immensity. She felt like Calista, she felt the inner strength of being a giant bear. Was it all in her head? Did she look like a bear too? She took a long, deep breath, closed her eyes, and another long breath. With a mighty groan, she sat straight up and people scattered as she pushed the machine off her chest like it was a twig.

"She's alive! Emilia! Calista! They're alive!" someone shouted. A thundering cheer went up throughout the crowd.

Her insides and outsides were tangled and mingled together. She was Calista, yet she remained Emilia, only stronger. Much stronger. Invincible! The enormity, tranquility, and strength of the body and spirit of Calista lived inside of her. Though she did not fully understand it, she could feel it and no longer questioned or feared it. She knew that she was the Biggest Bear for as long as she believed she was.

14 – ASHES TO ART

With the help of her family, Emilia was able to rise and steady herself. The crowd buzzed like swarming bees. Some examined the wreckage, most were watching Emilia, talking quietly to each other. She stood slowly, working to regain her balance in what felt like an unfamiliar body. People moved away, in part to give them some space, but also because the awe of what they had just witnessed and the full impact of the impossible sight before them were starting to sink in.

"I believe this is yours, my queen?" A sparkling Anzi bowed from within a lightning storm and handed her the Staff he had caught when it fell from her hand.

"That tingles," they said in unison as the lightning transferred from one to the other; and again in unison they laughed.

Standing tall and straight, she tapped the staff on the ground. It felt good, it felt solid, and like a long-forgotten memory, it felt like hers.

"Where's Miguel?" Emilia asked, stretching her neck.

Mama looked around, concerned. "I haven't seen him since we got here. Last I saw he was running after you!"

Alonso and his mother now joined them. Gabriela wasted no time in embracing Emilia. With her hands on Emilia's shoulders, she looked her intensely in the eyes. "Your grandmother would be *very* proud of you!"

The comment filled Emilia with a mix of love and pride. She knew Gabriela's statement to be true, and she was in turn proud of the grandmother she knew only through glimpses of time and memory. She hugged Gabriela close. "Please, tell me *all* about her!" said Emilia.

"Nothing would make me happier!" Gabriela beamed.

Alonso and Ernesto embraced briefly with slaps on the back, then quickly took charge by gathering a group to confront the Caláco workers, who were still guarding their machines. With no direction, nowhere to go, and no way to get there, the workers could only watch things unfold with everyone else in equal disbelief.

Emilia could still see everything clearly mapped out in her mind. From that vantage point, she was able to keep a close eye on her father's movement toward Tode's crew. Some of them still held guns, ready to protect themselves and their equipment. Emilia closed her eyes in concentration, tapped the Staff twice on the ground, and heard a cascade of thuds as all the guns fell out of their limp hands just as Papa and his team arrived. Surrounded and unable to operate their hands enough to pick up the weapons, the tables were now turned against Caláco's men. Emilia giggled in surprise that her thought experiment actually worked.

"No more guns! No more tricks!" shouted Alonso, picking up the dropped weapons and emptying them. There was no time to question the magic they were witnessing but were grateful for its timely arrival. And there was definitely no more need for guns.

"Into the bucket! All of you!" Ernesto ordered. The bucket attached to the long arm of the machine was big enough to hold a dozen men. Caláco's team realized they were hopelessly outnumbered and reluctantly climbed into the machine's bucket without a struggle. "Where's your fearless leader?" he asked them.

"Tode?" one of them replied with venom in his voice, "He's calling in reinforcements! You'll all be sorry!"

Alonso quickly climbed up into the cab, started the engine and hit the control to lift the bucket of destruction high into the air, swinging it just enough to make the men a little nervous about their immediate future. The engine sputtered to a stop.

"Sorry, fellas, it stalled out. You guys should really maintain your equipment a little better!" Alonso called up to the captives. He climbed down to the ground and shared a brief laugh and mutual slaps on the back, while the men in the bucket groaned and hurled curses from above.

"Don't be mad," joked Ernesto, "you can take this time to get to know each other better. Be good bucket-buddies now!"

Mama saw him first. Tode scurried along the outside edge of the crowd, crouched low, chin down, trying to hide within the commotion and get to the street unnoticed. His jacket was open and flapped behind him as he moved. He wasn't very far away.

In a single, silent motion, Arely leapt, spun in mid-air, and landed like a cat. She took a single step forward, planted her right knee on the ground, reached to her right ankle and pulled her throwing knife up and around. The knife released from her hand, twirling end over end through the air until finally, with pinpoint accuracy and force, it caught the back of Tode's jacket and pinned him to the tree he was running past. He lurched backward, let out a shout and fell to the ground. With the wind knocked out of him, he struggled in vain to get free of his jacket.

"NEVER" Mama stood over him and roared, "again will you harm my family!"

Tode was immediately surrounded by a crowd including Mama, Anzi, Gabriela, and Emilia.

"He's mine," said Emilia calmly and confidently. Her inner Bear was instantly available, giving her the strength and height required to pick him up single-handedly by the front of his jacket. The jacket tore away from the knife still lodged in the tree. She lifted Tode high enough to look him in the eye and snorted. It's all she needed to do. The front of Tode's pants suddenly became wet. She walked him over to the bucket that held his crew and tossed him just exactly right to land him in the perch with the others.

Ernesto and Alonso looked at each other in shock, then at Emilia, back up at the men, then at each other again, still wide-eyed, and burst into laughter and cheers along with everyone else.

Emilia brushed her hands together and turned toward the road where distant shouting was getting louder. Strangely, she could see over the heads of everyone, all the way to the other side of the crowd with her new-found map-vision.

"I see them! Papa! Over there!" called Emilia, pointing. "It's Miguel, and... Toro?" They ran in the direction she pointed. Mama stayed by her side. Anzi held Emilia's arm and Gabriela held his.

The boys were running after several older men. The older men dove into the back of a waiting car and slammed the doors. It was sleek, shiny, long, and black, with lots of chrome. In the driver's seat was Bigly III. The car's engine raced and the tires slung dirt into the air, confounding the boys. Then the engine choked and slowed. Emilia raised Calista's Staff, closed her eyes in concentration, and thumped the Staff on the ground. The car bounced to a stop with four flat tires, a loud bang, and smoke pouring from the engine. The men jumped out of the car and ran, with the boys again in pursuit.

Another car appeared in the distance, speeding down the street. It screeched to a stop and more men spilled out of it, joining the boys in the chase. Emilia did not recognize any of them. Ernesto and Alonso led yet another group in the chase. "Get them! Don't let them get away!" they shouted. Everyone ran to the street, swept up in the excitement but still a little nervous about the possibility of more violence.

A man from within the running Caláco gang turned around. The boys saw the gun and dove for cover just before the shots were fired. The crowd jeered. Emilia raised her Staff again, then thumped it firmly on the ground. She was acting on instincts that surprised her, but she held back her questioning mind to work with the Staff and the urgency at hand. When her Staff hit the ground, the men with guns screamed in pain, dropping their searing, red-hot weapons. Everyone stopped, but only briefly, stunned to see the guns melt into puddles of molten metal on the ground, but the commotion quickly resumed.

Emilia looked at her mother, shook her head, rolled her eyes, and smirked. "Ay. Men." She thought she was whispering, but her whisper seemed to have vanished. Mama laughed with delight and surprise, despite the dire situation, making Emilia laugh a hearty laugh that turned to a deep roar, which made them both open their eyes wide with surprise, and made Emilia cover her mouth as if she had just burped loudly. Then all four of them started laughing, but not for long.

Emilia concentrated and flicked her Staff. This time a little spark flew off the top where the bear head was carved. Bigly III and the other Caláco men being chased, tripped and fell to the ground where they were quickly and easily apprehended by Miguel, Toro, and his gang. The men from the other car swooped in to help hold them, followed by more of the crowd, followed in turn by a deafening cheer of victory.

Toro lifted his hands over his head and clasped them together in triumph, then took a dramatic bow. Pug and the rest followed his lead to the crowd's continued cheers. Miguel took no bow, but instead playfully pushed Toro on the shoulder, knocking him off balance and shoving him into Pug, who pushed him back. Toro took a step to the side, caught his balance, and looked at Miguel, both their faces wide with surprise. In one tense moment, Toro clenched his hand causing Miguel to flinch but then stand tall. Toro lifted his arm high over his head, Miguel did the same, and their hands slapped together in a solid high-five!

Ernesto and Alonso pushed their way quickly in between the men, boys, friends, and foes. Emilia, Anzi, Arely, and Gabriela moved more slowly through the mass of cheering people, not feeling the need to do anything except keep their arms around each other. Emilia held Calista's Staff high as the four of them moved with poise and conviction to stand with Ernesto and Alonso, who now had a firm grip on Bigly III. Everyone quieted and stepped aside to let them through.

Anzi spoke directly to Bigly III. "You and your predecessors made promises to us and our fathers many years ago. Included was the promise that you would bring a better life to our village. Is that what you call this?" He swept his arms across their path of ruin.

Ernesto lifted his authoritative voice. "Now is your time to make good on those promises. You can start with this mess, and you can start now." Bigly and his crew were heavily outnumbered, had no weapons, no transportation, and no choice.

The crowd burst out cheering and chanting, "*Take back the bear! Take back the bear!*" They had just witnessed a narrowly averted disastrous future, still unaware of all the details, and of how the distant past unfolded onto the solid ground of now.

Ernesto took the lead to escort Bigly III, while Alonso took a group to the machines to retrieve Tode and the rest of the Caláco crew. They lowered the bucket-buddies and brought them to the rubble pile that was once the bandstand. Surrounded and defenseless, the crew began picking up broken boards and stacking them in piles.

Miguel finally caught up to Emilia. "You're beautiful!" he said.

"*Miguel!*" She threw her arms around him, stepping out of her family circle. "I can't wait to tell you everything!" she spoke into his ear, then stood back exclaiming, "But Toro? Really? You and Toro and Pug and the rest of them? You were working *together?*"

"I can't wait to tell *you* everything!" he said with a confidence neither of them had ever heard.

Whatever happened, whatever she was, whatever she looked like, she was still, and always would be Emilia to him, and he would always love her.

"Hey! Cut it out, *lovebirds!*" Toro suddenly appeared and playfully bashed into both of them with his shoulder, bouncing off Emilia, who didn't even flinch. "Ow, hey!" he called out, rubbing his arm, "That hurt!" He paused, lowered his eyes and changed his tone to sincerity, "Thanks, Emilia."

"Yo, tell us the story about that bear myth!" called Pug, as he and the others quickly joined the group.

"I can't wait to tell everyone everything!" boomed Emilia, "But first we need to have a party!"

"*Take back the bear!*" the boys all shouted in unison. They put their arms around each other's shoulders and marched off chanting through the crowd. The singing, chanting, shouting, human chain grew in length and before long the entire party had been moved from Emilia's house to the park. Many carts arrived bringing all the food and decorations to the place where the feast once was and from now on, would always be.

One of the men who had been in the second car walked steadily, heading straight to Anzi and looking very determined. He was older, but not quite as old as Anzi, and wore a white suit that was a bit worse for wear after the chasing and tackling he had just been through. Emilia didn't recognize him and stepped in front of her grandfather as he approached. She folded her arms, narrowed her eyes, and instinctively gritted her teeth fiercely. Nobody would ever have a chance to hurt him again as long as she was alive. Anzi shot her a smiling spark, squeezed her hand, and let go. She let the stranger pass but stood close. Anzi embraced him heartily.

"Not a moment too soon, Tomás! It is good to see you, my old friend!"

"Indeed it is! I'm glad that old radio is still working for you, Manuel, and that you were able to contact me. You know I've kept up with the events of your village over the years. Quite dramatic I'd say! Not exactly the fiesta I expected from your invitation."

"Nor I. At least, not entirely," Anzi smiled and gestured to Emilia. "This is my granddaughter, our remarkable Emilia."

"My honor to meet you, Emilia," said Tom.

She politely but silently shook his hand. He was much older but she now recognized him from the vision Anzi shared with her, yet she was still on high alert for possible danger. Hearing someone call him Manuel seemed odd but reminded her again that her grandfather had a long life, long before hers even started.

"Perhaps this will be a nice research project for you?" Anzi said.

"Ha! No!" replied Tom. "Many years ago, perhaps. This is entirely a pleasure trip. In fact, we've been looking for a quiet place to retire, but I see it is perhaps not so quiet here!" He turned and drew his companion toward him. "Manuel, please meet my wife, Rose."

"Ah, Rose! A pleasure indeed!" Anzi embraced her, casting a wink to Tom as he did.

Tom gripped Anzi's arm with both hands saying, "It is good to see you, Manuel. You know, I've reviewed your contract with Caláco on our new electronic data transfer system."

"You did what? On the what? I do not understand."

"I'll explain later. But we now have retroactive anti-coercion laws that will protect your village legally, and ultimately reimburse you for damages. A bloody mark does not hold up in any court of law as a legal signature. There is nothing for you to worry about legally. And, to your concern that we spoke of by radio, I see no reason why you can't retain traditions while keeping your community active in the modern world. I would be happy to help navigate this with you."

"Ah, well, thank you again, Tomás. I wish I had not been so over-confident when you offered your help so long ago. But I am not worried, nor again am I the right person for you to speak with. Later I will introduce you to my son Ernesto and his wife Arely. You will, of course, stay with us!"

"Oh, no, we couldn't..." Tom started.

"Please do not offend an old man!" Anzi held up his hand to stop him. "There is plenty of room for you both. For now, welcome to our Bella Luna celebration! A very special year indeed to honor the return of our beautiful Calista!" he turned, extending his arm and bowing his head to Emilia. "There is so much food! I recommend the soup and bread!" He pointed to the line around the long food table which had been fashioned on the spot from the remains of the bandstand. "I will look for you there in a few minutes. Now go and enjoy yourselves!"

With smiles and nods, they turned to get some food and joined the crowd by the bonfire that was now roaring to life; a sad but reverent farewell to the remainder of the old bandstand.

"What has happened to me?" There was finally a moment for Emilia to speak with her grandfather.

"You have grown up, young lady, you said 'Yes'!" He held both her hands in his as he spoke and looked at them. "They are much bigger than they were just a few short hours ago!" he chuckled. "Look at what *yes* can do, not just for you but for your family, your village, your future! Everyone's future!" He swept his hands across the crowd, "For hope. You have earned what you most desired by accepting the challenges given to you. It is a great honor to be chosen as you have, an honor bestowed only upon those with a pure heart, those who can see with a sight beyond eyes."

"But I'm just me." She looked her body up and down, stretching out her limbs, "Whatever that is." Her arms seemed to be fuzzily fading between large and furry, and normal. "Can everyone see this or is it just me?"

"You are still Emilia, you always will be. And you will always be Calista for as long as you honor that part of you by saying *yes* to your truest passion in *every* moment, to make every *next* moment the most and best that it can be. You are much needed to be the creative expression of the art of you!"

"The art of me?"

"You. The animated, living art you have become will be interpreted now by those who see, reflected in you, the beauty, power, and hope that lives in them."

"I know it's not for me anymore, but I think it would be easier to be a little brown bean," she confided. "How can I be all of these things at once?"

"The one can only be heard with the ringing of the two."

"Anziiii..." she rolled her eyes, then closed them, smiled, shook her head. "I," she took a deep breath, "I think I get it. I guess maybe I'll have to think about that one."

"Do not think too hard! Only your heart can hear *that* sound."

She reached down to the torn, red tyet. "I'm sorry, I lost the pouch you gave me! And all the teeth! Maybe I can still find some of them!"

"You do not need your baby teeth anymore! You have everything you need right here." He placed one of his palms on her back, the other on her front, warming her insides. "Including the memory of when you needed those old teeth, and how losing them gave you the courage you needed to grow out of them."

"And I couldn't have done *any* of it without *you!*"

"Reflections! The soil needs water from the clouds, trees need a direction to grow, the artist's canvas needs another's eye to behold it, and a song needs an ear. We are all reflections of reality for one another. We cannot come alive without them."

"I *get* that one!" she straightened her spine and pointed her index finger straight up. She momentarily examined a long, pointed fingernail and gave it a little twang with another nail. "This is so weird," she quickly changed the subject. "Do you think there are enough of your friends who remember everything? We seriously need to rebuild this place and we'll need some stories while we work!"

"Well, young lady," he smiled, "I should think that with all the energy you and your young friends have, combined with our new machinery and skilled labor, and whatever mumbo-jumbo Tomás was talking about, we will make quick work of rebuilding. It would be good to collect and record our history."

"Mumbo-jumbo?" Emilia laughed. "Seriously? Where did *that* come from?"

"I like to keep up with the latest things you young people say!"

Emilia rolled her eyes and groaned.

"But I leave it to you and your friends to transform these ashes into art. That task will need a strong leader," said Anzi.

"Ashes to art. I like that!" she twinkled at him. Her belly groaned. She rubbed it, looked over at the food table and added, "I'm hungry!" Her voice dropped to a low roar as she said it and she quickly covered her mouth.

Anzi reached into his bag and pulled out a small jar of honey, handing it to her with a wide grin. She took it and started giggling, then he started chuckling, and soon they were both laughing long and loud.

Regaining a small amount of composure, Emilia asked, "You knew?"

"Of course!" Anzi winked.

She tipped the jar and poured the honey into her mouth, every last drop, and she grew again; Emilia into Calista. She put her arm around her grandfather and squeezed him tightly.

"Careful now, Calista, these old bones do not take well to bear hugs!" He returned her squeeze with a strength that made her wince with surprise. They each turned, looking the other in the eyes, eyes that sparkled, like magic.

EPILOGUE

Late into the night, when the work and fun of the day was finished, when the fire had turned to ash and all had gone home to tell and retell the stories, imagine the future, and recount the miracles of the day until their eyes grew so heavy they could no longer keep them open, only then in the quiet, covered, stillness of dark that comes just before dawn, did the moon open her eyes. And when she did, and she saw what had happened this day, she gleamed a little brighter and gained a bit of round. Each of the lost teeth glistened in the soil under her milky white light and by sunrise they were gone, a circle of 20 strong trees standing in their place. Within this henge, a new future had already taken root.

If you liked The Biggest Bear, please leave a review on your favorite review site. Reviews make a big difference to both authors and readers!

Engage with the author
www.sunlightning.com

Follow the Bear on Facebook
https://www.facebook.com/PaulJAuthor

Be the Bear!

FROM THE AUTHOR

The seed for *The Biggest Bear* came from a dream. When writing the story, I imagined the bullies I faced, the conflicts in the news every day, people oppressed by political leaders, poverty, circumstance, and just plain bad luck. And then I imagined that there was a way to receive infinite support from a place of infinite knowing. In this story, that knowing is embodied in Anzi. In reality, it can only come from deep within the most fearless part of yourself – like the "Tank Man" of Tiananmen Square in 1989 – the part that can either free you or kill you, but either way will change your life and the lives of others. Anzi can't say 'yes' for Emilia, she has to do that for herself. We can never *really* know though – the best we can do is learn to trust, to dance in the dark. Often, all it takes is a hand on your shoulder and the words, "Yes, you can!"

If you don't have that hand on your shoulder for whatever reason, you can use Emilia's. She's got big hands! Or are they paws? When you rise to each challenge, you are the bear! I hope you'll share your own "bear story" of how you rose to a challenge that changed you. Share it with a friend, or someone you don't know who might need that share.

I love the fiery passion I feel when traveling in Latin America, and it plays into the telling of this story; as does my belief that masculine and feminine aspects need to be in balance. They are clearly out of balance at this point in history, and I hope that Emilia's story helps empower the feminine aspect embedded within all of us. When I first visited Mexico, I was astounded that there were coffee fields everywhere but the only kind of coffee I could buy was powdered instant. The beans were sold away from the places where they grew, then processed and shipped back to the growers in the form of the least appealing product that can be made from the raw material. This kind of thing happens all over the world – maybe even right where you live. That was my first, first-hand lesson about the oppression of global economics and corporate control. Precious few places remain in the world where nature provides for and supports humans directly with food, water, shelter, medicine, and the freedom of creative self-expression. We have lost much, as a species, at the hands of those who play with power and like to control others. We all have a "Caláco" in our life: a bully, an oppressor, a self-image, a knee on our neck, a thing that prevents us from saying 'yes' to the gifts that we know we have.

I try to offer a more grounded view of a very tangled world, something based on what we all feel deeply, rather than what we react to superficially. I think we humans strive for some ultimate, authentic relationship to others, and we can share ourselves through our work, music, stories, dance, art, writing, or any creative force that makes us feel truly alive inside, even just being a good friend is a creative act.

Today, I'm grateful to live quietly off the grid, surrounded by nature where various bits of news, observations, musings, insights, and dreams sometimes coalesce into a coherent story. My writing explores the alternating tension, fear, connection, passion, and insecurity we all feel. Our best is borne of personal struggle, internal or external, mixed with the honest desire to create something for all to enjoy and benefit from.

Please visit and share your thoughts at
www.sunlightning.com

Made in United States
North Haven, CT
08 July 2023

38690514R10088